CROSS CHECKED

A HAT TRICK NOVELLA

MADI DANIELLE

Copyright © 2024 by Madi Danielle

All rights reserved.

No part of this book may be reproduced in any form or by any electronic or mechanical means, including information storage and retrieval systems, without written permission from the author, except for the use of brief quotations in a book review.

This novel is entirely a work of fiction. The names, characters and incidents portrayed in it are the work of the author's imagination. Any resemblance to actual persons, living or dead, events or localities is entirely coincidental.

Designations used by companies to distinguish their products are often claimed as trademarks. All brand names and product names used in this book and on its cover are trade names, service marks, trademarks and registered trademarks of their respective owners. The publishers and the book are not associated with any product or vendor mentioned in this book. None of the companies referenced within the book have endorsed the book.

Cover Design: Aliyah with Forever Star Cover Design.

Editing: Kay with KMorton Editing Services.

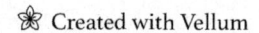

❦ Created with Vellum

PLAYLIST

Plot line – Emlyn
Seven – Natalie Jane
Only Forever – Demi Lovato
Stop Fighting It - April Jai
Is It Over Now? (Taylor's Version) – Taylor Swift
Dirty Little Dream – RAINNE
Plastic palm trees – Tate McRae
CITY OF ANGELS – Demi Lovato

*To those of you that want a man to respect you outside the bedroom.
But disrespect the fuck out of you inside it.*

FOREWORD

This is a fun, spicy story that I wrote purely for the vibes. There's little plot to be had here so don't be expecting much of it. Just grab a toy (you know the kind), maybe some wine, and *enjoy.*

It is recommended to read The Hat Trick before this, but not required. If you have, the timeline for this novella is two years after the events of The Hat Trick.

1

SPENCER

I'm covered in sweat, breathing hard, my auburn hair is sticking to my forehead and neck making me itchy. Yet, this is when I feel the best. Getting off stage. The high I feel after performing for so many people is wild. The crowd singing along with me, knowing *my* lyrics. Nothing in this world has ever felt better.

"You were amazing, as always," my friend and publicist, Brynn Collee, beams.

"Thanks," I smile, taking the towel she hands me to wipe off the sweat. It doesn't matter that I'm performing in Colorado in the dead of winter, stage lights get hot. Plus, all the fire I incorporate into my shows because of my namesake. *Spencer Sparks*. No, it's not a stage name, yes this is what my parents named me.

"You also got your nightly message from the bestie, and some social media notification from the boyfriend," Brynn relays while handing over my phone.

I smile at the message from my best friend, Jared. We grew up next door to each other in New York and have always been close. He's a goalie for the Denver Dragons and it's become a routine for us to text each other before our respective jobs. Him before I perform and me before his games.

> Jared: Good luck tonight, sing your lungs out. Except not literally because you're too young for retirement.

Next, I roll my eyes at the social media notification from my boyfriend, Kenneth. Not Ken. Not Kenny. *Kenneth.* Because that's the only thing anyone is allowed to call him. He tagged me in a picture we took over a month ago, the caption is basic just like him. We've been having issues lately, especially with me being on tour and him in season because he is *also* a hockey player. It's like they are drawn to me or something, at least that's what Brynn always jokes about.

Kenneth and I met two years ago when I sang the national anthem before one of his games with the L.A. Spartans. He insisted on finding me after the game and taking me out and the rest is history. He was sweet, I really liked him, but over the last few months his true colors have come out. Or maybe I was blind to it the whole time, I'm not sure. Either way, it seems like the more well-known I became, the worse he treated me.

Of course, on social media it's all about image which he is trying to keep looking pristine. Can't show any indication that he screamed at me over the phone last night. No, Kenneth Richardson has to look perfect to the world.

At one time he looked perfect to me too. Now, not so much.

I ignore the picture he posted without liking, leaving a

comment or reposting it. I know this will be another fight, but I don't care. I'm on the high from performing and I intend to keep it that way.

"Are we still going to the game tomorrow?" Brynn asks as we walk back to the dressing room so I can change out of my sweat-soaked outfit.

"Hell yeah we are." We decided to stay an extra day in Colorado to see a game since Brynn's brother, Brent, and my friend Jared play on the same team.

"Good because if you said no, I was going to stay here and go to it without you."

"You know I would never do that to you," I tell her as I'm already peeling off the sticky fabric from my body in my dressing room.

"You never told me what happened with douche – I mean Kenneth last night."

I scoff. Brynn has never been a huge fan of my boyfriend, but since our relationship has gotten worse, so has her opinion of him. Of course, she gets to see first-hand how he treats me a lot of the time and she's not impressed.

"Same shit, different day. We fought, he yelled, we hung up. He texted a half assed apology, then goes on to post something with us when he hasn't spoken to me since."

"When are you going to dump the asshole?"

I finish taking off my clothes and am pulling on some

sweatpants and a sweatshirt while I consider what she said. Of course, I've thought about breaking up with Kenneth, especially lately, but honestly I'm worried about what he might do.

Sighing, I answer the only way I know how, "Soon."

She looks at me like she knows I don't mean it but doesn't say anything else. We've been friends since we met freshman year in college and instantly clicked. We've been inseparable since, which is how I think we are able to communicate without saying anything sometimes. She's stuck by me through everything from when I started posting videos of myself singing on YouTube, to recording my first album. Lucky for both of us she studied public relations, so when I was told to hire a publicist it was a no brainer.

Once we are back to the hotel we separate to our own rooms, and I instantly call Jared. We talk in some way every day, sometimes it's just texts and other times it's a phone or FaceTime call. We promised to be friends forever a long time ago and we both have made sure to maintain that.

"Hey Superstar," he greets.

"Hey puck stopper."

"How was the show tonight?"

"You would know if you were there," I joke, though I was disappointed to learn that Jared's team had an away game tonight before coming back for a home game tomorrow.

"Not my fault. I don't make the game schedule," he defends.

"I know, but you owe me, especially since I'm coming to your game tomorrow."

He chuckles, "I know. I promise to come to one soon."

"You better, you know a promise is a serious commitment. You don't just get to break those."

"I would never." His tone changes, "I saw *Kenneth's* post. How's that going?"

Jared doesn't like Kenneth. Never has, said he's an asshole ever since we started dating and I defended him for a while, but just like my entire relationship, it's getting harder and harder to do.

I sigh. "I think that post was him trying to gaslight the world that everything is fine, but we got in yet another fight last night and I'm just getting sick of it."

Jared hums, I know he holds back from telling me to dump his ass, which in some ways I appreciate. Other times I wish he would be blunt like Brynn and try to convince me to bite the bullet. "What was the fight about?" he finally asks.

"Honestly, I don't even know anymore." I really don't. Whatever it was I'm sure I was blamed, but it always ends the same. With him telling me that I need him. I even used to believe that bull shit. Not anymore, though.

"Hm," he hums again.

"What?" I say on a humorless laugh.

"I don't get it, Spence. You could do so much better than that asshole. I don't get why you stay with him."

"I know," it's all I can say without crying.

"I'm sorry."

I clear my throat. "Don't be sorry, there's nothing for you to be sorry about. I know it's my mess I have to deal with."

"I know you will," there's a softness in his voice now and it only makes the possibility of tears higher.

"I'm exhausted, I'm going to go to sleep. Can't wait to see you tomorrow." I try to sound cheery, but I don't think I convince him.

"See you tomorrow, Superstar."

We hang up and instead of going to sleep I pull out my song writing notebook. I've tried using my phone, computer, or tablet for writing, but nothing compares to good 'ol pen and paper. It's how I do my best work.

I end up writing a mess of lyrics and melodies until the sunlight starts shining through the windows. Even though what I'm writing may never turn into anything it's obvious who it's inspired by. And it's not the guy who is supposed to be my boyfriend.

2

COLVER
30

I don't know if I should believe what I'm looking at. Tabloids and gossip sites make shit up all the time. The number of rumors I've seen about Spencer over the years that I've asked her about, only to be met with hysterical laughter is too many to count.

There's something about this one that rings true. Maybe it's the conversation we had last night that gives me hope. Or it's the quote that is supposedly right from *Kenneth*. That fucking asshat. He's not only a dirty player on the ice, he's also just a shit person. I've seen it from when he and Spencer first started dating, but she couldn't. I never wanted her relationship to be the reason our friendship suffers so I hold back. For the most part.

Sparks' Romance Fizzles Out
Sources say Spencer Sparks and L.A. Spartans player Kenneth Richardson end their two-year relationship.

Maybe she finally dumped his ass after we got off the phone yesterday. I sent her a text, even though I wanted to call her. I don't want her to possibly hear how excited I am that this is true.

> Jared: Hey, I just saw this. Is it true?

I add a link to the article to the text, then start getting ready to head to the practice facility for morning skate. We had an away game yesterday afternoon and flew home right after. I was hoping we would be back in time for me to go to Spencer's concert, but we weren't so I went home instead.

Once I'm pulling into the parking lot at the practice arena, I check my phone one more time and there isn't a response from Spencer, so I throw it in my bag and head in for practice.

The coaches go easy on all of us at practice since we are doing back to backs and don't want to risk over exhaustion or any injuries. We end practice with a short scrimmage, and I can tell everyone is taking it easy because none of them get a single goal past me.

I'm showered and heading out the door when I decide to check my phone again. There are several messages from Spencer, all timed a few minutes apart like she was giving me a play-by-play as she processed what I sent her. Safe to say she did not know about it.

> Spencer: What the fuck?
> Spencer: That snake.

> Spencer: I'm going to kill him. And no that's not permission for you to kill him. I want to do it. With my bare hands. Or maybe I'll use a weapon.
>
> Spencer: Can I borrow a skate blade or two?
>
> Spencer: Brynn is running damage control.

I call her as soon as I get into my car. She answers almost frantically like she's been running around all morning, "Hey."

"Hey. You okay?"

"Yeah, oh yeah, I'm great. Never better, really. Hey, do you think it would be better to hide a body in the ocean or to burn it?"

I can't help but laugh. "Probably burn it first then hide all the evidence in the ocean."

"You're a genius. And officially an accomplice so don't think about going to the cops."

"I would never," I bite back my laugh. "But seriously, you okay? What happened?"

"Brynn has been trying to figure it out, but from what it looks like, Kenneth went to the press, said we broke up. Played up how heartbroken he is and is now ignoring me."

"That motherfucker," I practically growl.

"I know. I mean, I'm not exactly sad about it, but I am pretty pissed that he's making me look like shit and that he's the scorned ex. Oh my god, I'm going to *kill him!*"

"I think you're pretty deep in your murder thoughts. I get it, I do, but I really want to make sure you're okay."

She sighs, "Yeah, I'm not like sad or anything if that's what you're asking."

That was what I was asking. I don't want her crying over that piece of shit, he doesn't deserve it. If she wants to be angry, that is something I can get behind.

"Good. Let's do something after the game tonight to make you feel better that won't end with us in prison for twenty-five to life."

"That's only if we get caught, and I don't plan on getting caught," she says, deadpan.

"Okay, killer, what do you say?"

"Yeah, okay. What did you have in mind?"

"Not sure yet, I'll figure it out. Write some songs or something in the meantime." I know songwriting has always been her best outlet, which is why she's so successful now. Spencer Sparks is extremely talented. Not only is her voice absolute perfection, but her talent with writing songs is unmatched. She does a blend of pop and rock that is completely unique to her.

"Okay. Thank you, Jared."

I smile as we hang up. Next, I have an idea on what we can do, but I have to make some calls first.

BACK-TO-BACK GAMES ARE hard on everyone. The entire team is slower than usual, and I'll admit so am I. Luckily, I haven't let in any goals yet, but it's been close. We haven't scored anything either by the end of the second period.

The zero-zero score has everyone a bit more fired up as we return to the ice for the third and final period. No one wants to go into overtime, and no one wants to lose either. Our opponents are also fired up as a few of the guys start playing a bit dirtier than they should. Hard hits, chirping shit at my teammates to try and get them to draw a penalty. Some guys even daring to skate too close to me.

We are about halfway through the period when I let a goal past me on a fake out, my weakness, if I'm being honest. The other team celebrates while I skate in a frustrated circle. It was a textbook fake out and yet it worked on me. I'm sure they have watched tape and know that's where I lack. I'm still pissed about it.

I don't let anymore through, but neither does the other goalie so we end up losing on a single goal. Which only makes me feel shittier about it.

My teammate and captain, Collee, pats my shoulder pads while we head back to the locker room, "It's okay, that was a tough game."

"We got shut out."

He shrugs, "It was just one goal."

"Yeah, one goal *I* missed."

"Shake it off, it's early in the season, it's not like we just lost the Cup."

"I know. Thanks, man."

Collee nods and we go our separate ways in the locker room. Some of my frustration tonight has nothing to do with the game and more to do with what Spencer has had to spend her day dealing with. I know what I have planned for us is something we both need.

We meet up in the tunnel after I'm showered and changed back into my game day suit. Spencer is standing with a couple of my teammate's girlfriends, Chandler and Audrey. Collee is pulling his sister, Brynn, in for a hug when I approach. Spencer wraps her arms around me in a way I didn't realize I desperately needed.

"Hey Superstar," I say against the top of her head.

She looks up at me with her chin against my chest, keeping her arms around me. "Sorry you lost."

"Damn, you know I almost forgot about that and then you just had to remind me."

She rolls her eyes, pulling her arms off my torso and whacking my chest with the back of her hand lightly. I miss the warmth of her pressed against me almost instantly. Spencer has always been touchy with me, and I've always enjoyed it. More so in recent years, the older we get the more the soft press of her body against mine feels like it could possibly mean *more*.

But we are friends. We've always been friends and nothing more. Even if I've wanted that to change.

"Did you come up with what you wanted to do?" she asks.

I nod. "Yup. Was Brynn wanting to come with?"

I cross my fingers secretly, hoping she says no.

"I'm not sure." She turns to Brynn and asks.

"No thanks, I'm going to hang out with my brother. And by that, I mean his girlfriend," she answers with a chuckle.

"You miss me, don't try to pretend," Collee yanks Brynn against his side and shaking her until she's pushing him away. His girlfriend, Chandler, just laughs.

It doesn't take long until we are joined by Vince Dumont and Matt McQuaid who are also dating Chandler. It's a complicated dynamic to me, but they make it work and I've never seen four people so happy. Well, most of the time. McQuaid is an obnoxious asshole and I know they all get into it at times.

Audrey is scooped up from behind by her boyfriend. She lets out a squeal when he twirls her around before setting her back on her feet and kissing her so hard, she bends backward, his arms the only things keeping her standing.

"You ready to head out, Sparks?" I ask, trying to take attention away from the affectionate couples I feel like we are completely surrounded by.

"Yeah, let's get out of here, Colver," turning to the group she says, "it was so nice to meet you, Chandler and Audrey."

"You too, feel free to join us whenever you have the time," Chandler beams.

"I'll see you tomorrow, remember we are going to have the plane ready at ten," Brynn says, wrapping Spencer in a hug.

"Got it. Colver won't keep me out past curfew, will you?" she winks up at me.

"I would never dream of it."

With some final waves we go to the parking lot, hopping into my black G wagon.

"Alright, where are we going, and do I need a hat or sunglasses?" she asks as I'm pulling out of the parking garage. It's a fair question, I know how famous she is and going out doing normal things isn't what it used to be with her. I might be well known in the hockey world, but it's rare anyone is stopping me on the street. With her it's constant.

"No hat needed; we have total privacy." I catch her smile at that, I don't think it's for the same reason I'm glad to have her alone. For her I think she likes when she can be herself without worrying about paparazzi or fans. "So, what ended up happening?"

She fidgets with the hem of her Denver Dragons t-Shirt she's wearing. I'm a little annoyed she's not wearing my jersey, but I'm not going to push it.

"Guess I'm single now. Brynn tracked down the 'source' which turned out to be Kenneth. He's actively ignoring any attempts I've made to talk to him so guess that means we are done." I watch her straighten in her seat, steeling herself like she usually does. Always having to appear strong and confident.

"Are you...okay?" I ask. I want to ask if she wants him back. I want to ask a million things that I'm choosing to combine into one word instead.

"Yup," she pops the P. "Saves me the effort of breaking up with him. And shows how much of a coward he really is."

I nod. "He's more than that, but we can stick with coward for now."

She laughs. I've always loved her laugh. It's like her voice when she sings, almost melodic like any noise that comes out of her mouth is going to be perfectly pitched without her even trying.

I bet the same can be said when she screams out as she orgasms.

Shit.

I try to keep those thoughts locked up as much as possible, knowing I'll never get to find out. Plus, we are friends. I shouldn't know that. I shouldn't *want* to know that. But I do.

Running my hand down my face like it can wipe the thoughts from my mind, she doesn't seem to notice my current internal dilemma of trying not to picture her naked underneath me and the noises she would make.

"So, where are we going?" she asks. Completely innocent. Safe territory.

I smile over at her, "You ready to break some shit?"

3

SPENCER

I've always found Jared attractive. I mean who wouldn't? He's a six foot two hockey goalie with dark brown hair and the brightest blue eyes I've ever seen. Plus, I know he's hiding a perfectly sculpted body under the suit he's currently wearing. The suit that I've wanted to rip off since I saw him.

But we are friends.

I just got dumped, very publicly.

And Jared has never indicated he feels anything toward me other than friendship, which is fine. We've known each other for as long as I can remember, if anything was going to happen between us it would have by now. I accepted it long ago that my crush toward him would be unrequited.

He has no idea how many of my songs have been about him, either. And he never will because if he did then he would know how I really feel and...*nope*. Not going there.

He asked if I'm ready to break some shit. I didn't know he meant that literally until we are pulling into the parking lot of something called a rage room. The car turns off and he turns to me with his lips pulled into a wide, mischievous smile, "Ready?"

"Let's go break some shit," I practically leap out of the car toward the building.

We walk in to be greeted by a single employee whose eyes widen when they see us but appear to try and keep their cool.

"H-Hi," they clear their throat, "welcome, um it's just you two as requested."

I look up at Jared, unable to hold back my smile. I know it's inconvenient at times to deal with the complications that come with going out in public with me. The fact that he rented the place out just so I wouldn't have to worry about it makes me feel lots of things. Things I thought I've mostly buried and replaced with purely platonic feelings.

We are led back to a room with jumpsuits and goggles for safety, and the room for the raging is just through a door off to the side.

"Do you – uh – need anything else?" the employee asks, wringing their hands together nervously.

"No thank you, I think we can figure it out from here," Jared says, friendly as ever.

"Okay, yeah, cool. Just let me know if you do." They send

one final look my way with a blush on their cheeks before ducking their head and going back to the front.

"You know, if I didn't know you already, I would be afraid of you too. You're pretty scary looking," Jared teases once the employee is out of earshot.

I roll my eyes and smack his chest. "Whatever. You make your living by having actual weapons shot at you a hundred miles per hour. I'm not the scary looking one."

"Hey, I still have all my teeth at least!" he smiles wide to show off his perfectly straight, white teeth.

I laugh, shaking my head and grabbing a jumpsuit that is going to be too big on me and some goggles that are sure to leave indents in my skin.

Once we are dressed, we face each other and laugh at how ridiculous we both look. Then we go into the room, which is more like several rooms connected with empty door frames and a bunch of shit everywhere just waiting to be smashed.

There are some bats by the door for us to use as our weapon of choice and I almost laugh maniacally at the damage I'm about to inflict on some poor broken junk.

The first swing I take is on an old computer monitor which feels amazing, euphoric even. The glass shatters and I can't help but look up at Jared as he's watching me. I'm beaming, which I know he can see, and it only makes him meet my same energy.

"You joining me or just enjoying the view?" I ask, twirling

the bat around in a way I think looks cool, but probably doesn't at all.

"I was enjoying the view, but if you insist," with that, he takes a swing at a giant TV screen, and it instantly shatters at the force.

That was hotter than it should be.

I shake the thought away and go back to taking my aggression out. We make our way into other rooms with other objects, I like the one with all the glassware I get to throw and stomp on. The sound of glass shattering is extremely satisfying. Smashing an old window is also fun.

I'm not sure how much time passes as we get lost in destroying things, but I'm sweaty and breathing heavily when I pull up my goggles. Jared isn't far behind, doing the same. "You all done?" he asks.

"Yeah, I think I've wreaked enough havoc around here." I put my hands on my hips, proud of the destruction I've caused.

"Do you feel better?" Jared questions, closing the distance between us. I wrap my arms around his middle when he's close enough. I like touching him, I always have, and he never pushes me away.

Nodding, I reply, "Yeah, this was perfect. Thank you."

He rests his hands on my waist in a tentative touch and I feel my arms tighten around him. We are completely flush against each other, and the air feels charged. This isn't the first time I've felt this way. But it is the first time I'm wondering if one of us is going to cross the line we've always kept.

"You know I'd do anything for you, Spence," Jared says softly.

Our eyes are locked on each other, I'm not sure what to say. Not even sure I can say anything. It feels like we are leaning toward each other. I'm sure I'm hallucinating; I have to be because we are friends and that's how Jared has always seen me. He doesn't want to kiss me, *does he?*

Yet, it really feels like we are about to kiss. Especially when he raises his hand to cup my cheek, my eyes fall closed, my heart racing in my chest. I can't believe this is about to happen. I can feel his breath on my lips. I part them on instinct. I'm about to kiss Jared Colver. My best friend my entire life. The boy turned man I've always fantasized about. Always wanted. I can't believe I'm finally about to –

"Spencer," his low voice breaks me out of my thoughts as his forehead rests against mine.

I open my eyes, meeting the conflict in his. My cheeks burn in embarrassment.

"I want you to know that I want to kiss you. I really fucking do," he rasps, and I feel my knees buckle. "But I won't be a rebound for you. I can't. So, I need to know that you are in a good headspace before anything happens. Because once it does there's not a chance I can ever let you go."

My breath catches from his words. He wants to kiss me. He wants more than that. He doesn't want to be a rebound.

"Tell me you understand," he sounds almost pained and I'm realizing this is hard for him as well.

Instead of saying that, I spit out the only thing I can think of right now. "You want me?"

He lets out a humorless laugh. "Only since forever."

I step back, in shock from his words. He takes my movement as rejection, but I need the clarity that only can happen when my body isn't pressed against his.

"Why – " I lick my lips trying to piece together what I want to say. "Why have you never said anything before? Why now?"

He sighs. "Can we go somewhere else to talk about this where we aren't standing in a bunch of garbage?"

I look around like I'm remembering where we are. This revelation has me blinded to everything around us. Probably because I feel like I've been blind my whole life since I never saw any indication of this before now.

I nod, unable to say anything else. He guides me out with a hand on the small of my back while I'm reeling over the fact that I feel like my oldest friendship is about to burst into flames. The question remains, does that mean it's going to create an infinite inferno or burn to the ground so all that's left is ashes.

4

COLVER 30

Neither of us say anything as we change out of the dust covered jumpsuits and go back to my car. Tensions are thick, and I never intended for the night to turn this way, but watching her act so carefree as she smashed, crushed, and threw everything solidified my feelings that I've been suppressing for years. Her laugh echoing in those rooms while she let go has been everything.

Then she touched me, as she always does, but this time I couldn't help touching her back. I almost kissed her. I wanted to kiss her. But I can't do that, not unless I know she's mine and not just looking for an escape.

I drive us to the Red Rock Amphitheater. At this time, we are technically trespassing, but if we get caught I know they will let us go. Not to be cocky, but they know who I am and even if they don't, they definitely know who Spencer is.

"I want to perform here," she says, breaking the silence between us once I'm parked.

"I know, and you will. You're Spencer Sparks," I smile over at her.

She snorts a laugh, getting out of the car and I follow her.

We stand at the top of the amphitheater, taking it all in. The city lit up in the distance, down below. I want to pull her into my arms, but I can't. Not yet.

Finally, she turns toward me, arms folded across her chest. "Alright, Colver, explain."

I chuckle, taking her hand in mine so we can sit down on one of the rock seats and instead of letting her hand go, I wrap it in both of mine almost to make sure she won't yank it away.

"What do you want me to explain?" I know, but I want her to say it again.

"When did you start to feel...*something* for me? Why didn't you say anything? Why are you saying something *now?*" she rushes the words out like she can't speak them fast enough.

I sigh, running my hand through my hair. "I guess I started to feel...*something,*" I copy her wording in a sarcastic tone which results in her rolling her eyes and I chuckle. "Homecoming sophomore year."

Her brows furrow at that, and I continue. "That dickhead Mikey canceled on being your date last minute. Biggest mistake of his life, I'm sure. So, we went together and when I first saw you in that black dress, something switched within me. I've always thought you were pretty, but you were Spencer, my best friend. That night you became more, but I was a scared fifteen-year-old who didn't know what to do with all I was feeling. So, I did nothing."

"That was nine years ago," she states simply.

"Yeah, the more time went by the more I convinced myself it would be a bad idea to tell you in case you didn't feel the same way, then other relationships got in the way," I shrug. "I don't know, it never seemed like the right time."

"But it's the right time now?"

I chuckle. "No, probably not, but I refuse to let you slip through my fingers again. You have to know because I can't hold it in anymore. I also know that you just went through a very public breakup and are on tour so I understand that nothing can happen yet. But I just had to tell you."

She sighs, her hand tightening on mine. "Freshman year of high school."

I look at her, questioning what she's saying.

"That's when I realized I felt...*something*," she teases with a wink.

My jaw drops slightly as she continues. "I overheard some girls in our class talking about how hot you got over the summer and I realized I felt jealous. I spent almost every day with you that summer and I guess I didn't notice until I saw you again after hearing them. Then I saw it and I could never unsee it."

"Damn," I shake my head, realizing we've both been harboring our secret crushes on each other for years.

Spencer leans against me, resting her head on my shoulder as we continue to take in the view in front of us. I wrap my arm around her, and she melts into me just a little bit more. I want to kiss her. I don't think I've ever been so tempted to do anything in my life. But I meant what I said back at the rage room. I won't be a rebound for her, I can't.

Once I have a taste of her, I know it won't be enough. I'll need all of her.

"I looked at your schedule, you have a game in L.A. in two weeks," she says, breaking the silence between us.

I nod, I don't have the game schedule memorized by any means, so that is good to know. That reminds me to look up her show schedule so I can make sure to go to the soonest one. "Will you be there?"

"That's my plan, unless you don't want me to go."

I pull back, looking at her confused. "Of course I do."

She sends me a knowing smile, "Good, because I'd still be there even if you didn't want me to be."

My laughter tumbles out of me, and she joins in as I pull her back into me. We sit like that for a while, neither of us wanting the night to end. But I have a feeling that even when we are separated for these next two weeks, this isn't the end of *something*. It's the beginning of something new. Something exciting. Something I know is going to completely consume me.

～

As predicted the next two weeks drag. The highlight of every day is talking to Spencer. We've always talked a lot, maintaining our long-distance friendship has never been difficult for us. But this has been different. Subtle flirting, but never fully crossing the friendship line.

She has yet to mention anything about her relationship with Kenneth and I haven't seen any further tabloid stories about them. Either way, she doesn't seem too broken up about him and the loss of their relationship.

I know I'm about to see the asshole when we play against his team. And after the game I'm hoping to hang out with Spencer. And hope even more that she might be ready to take the leap with me. I realize it's still soon, but *God,* I want her.

This morning we are heading to L.A. and I'm excited and jittery. I'm the first one to the team plane and I'm silently cursing my teammates to hurry the fuck up so we can go.

"What's going on with you?" my teammate, Mann, asks as he takes the seat next to me.

"Huh? Nothing, just wanting to get on the road," I answer simply, looking around to see who on the team we are still missing and wondering if we can just leave without them. They can catch their own plane.

"I don't think I've ever seen anyone *excited* to go on a road trip," he throws me a suspicious look.

"My friend lives in L.A., so I guess I'm a little excited."

"Friend? Is that friend Spencer Sparks? Audrey is a big fan; she was very excited to tell me about hanging out with her at the game a couple weeks ago."

"Yeah, but she's not like that to me. She's just Spencer."

"You like her," Mann states. It's not a question.

"I might," I shrug like it's not a big deal.

Mann chuckles. "You don't have to downplay it. You're pretty fucking obvious right now. I hope you're going to go for it."

I wring my hands together in front of me. "It's complicated, her and her boyfriend of two years just broke up and I'm not going to be a rebound."

"Ah. I get that. But if you want something, go after it. Don't wait, trust me."

I nod at him. He's been with his girlfriend for a couple years now and I don't know the entire history between them. From what I understand there was some years before they got together officially, they talked and never met. I'm not sure entirely how that works, but Mann is close lipped on exactly how they met and how they got together.

We land in L.A. after about two and a half hours. I'm instantly texting Spencer.

> Jared: Landed in the city of angels.

> Spencer: Let me know if you see any, that might make a good song.

> Jared: Well, I know of one I'll get to see *wink emoji*

> Spencer: Omg STOP!

I chuckle, knowing I made her blush.

> Spencer: Are you doing anything tonight?

We don't play until tomorrow and I didn't want to push her to see me if she was already busy. Not only is she on tour already, but she also still writes and records songs in between stops. She's always been an overachiever. I swear she may not sleep.

> Jared: Other than getting my beauty rest, nope. Why? Are you wanting to see me, Ms. Sparks?

> Spencer: Ew, not if you call me the same thing you call my mom.

> Spencer: But yes.

> Jared: Me too. Send me your address and I'll come over after I get checked into my hotel.

She sends it to me instantly and now I'm back to being jittery and excited, wanting everyone to move faster to get off the plane.

After I'm checked into the hotel, I go to my room to toss my bag in and then I'm leaving again. Some of the guys were wanting to have a lowkey night getting dinner and some drinks at the hotel bar. I told them I probably wouldn't join them, and they all proceeded to give me shit about Spencer, but I don't care.

I take an Uber to her house that is tucked back in the Hollywood Hills, surrounded by a gate that security had to let me into. My driver asked what celebrity I was going to see, but I refused to tell him. He can figure out this is the house of a famous person, but he doesn't get to know it's Spencer.

I wait until the driver is out the gate before I walk up to the front door, not wanting to risk her being seen when she opens the door. Though, as soon as she does her wavy auburn hair is blown back by the wind. Her lips pull back into a wide smile I want to taste with my own mouth. She's in tight ripped high waisted jeans and a crop top that just shows a sliver of skin on her stomach. She launches at me, wrapping her arms around me.

"You're here," she breathes against my chest. I pull her tightly against me, feeling her relax in my hold as I walk us inside and shut her front door.

"I'm here," I smile against the top of her head.

She pulls back slightly to look up at me, her smile still so bright. "I've missed you."

"You have time to miss me?" I joke because I need to gauge where she is mentally before going any further. And if I admit I've been missing her like crazy that might open the flood gates to everything I've been feeling. Which will lead to touching her. Falling into her.

"Ha," she laughs once, pulling her arms off from around me and walking toward the living room with me following like a puppy dog. "I am great at multitasking so I'm able to miss you *and* do other things."

She flops down onto her large couch that sinks around my weight as I do the same. It's white and fluffy and feels like what I imagine a cloud feels like.

"How have you been?" I ask, like we haven't talked every single day. I angle my body toward her, resting my elbow on the back of the couch and propping my head on my fist.

She licks her lips and nods. "I've been good, actually. Better than I thought. Turns out I had about two hundred pounds of dead weight attached to me. Creating an expectation of me that I didn't want for myself. Weird how light I feel."

"That so?" I don't want her to just say what she thinks I want to hear. I want her truth, even if it's ugly.

"Yup. I've written more songs in the last two weeks than I think I have in the last month."

"Wow, can I hear any of them?"

She takes her bottom lip between her teeth, clearly nervous

for some reason. "There's one I, um, yeah. I wrote it after what you said about 'only since forever.' It inspired me."

"I want to hear it."

Spencer stands up, holding her hand out to me which I take so she can lead me into another room that has various instruments. I remember when she started taking piano lessons at first. She told me if she learned to play the piano, she could play any instrument and that was her mission. She learned the piano, guitar, and even the drums, though I don't think that one stuck.

Taking a seat at the piano I can feel her nervousness, though I'm not sure why. She's played songs for me before. That energy seems to fade as she plays the first few notes. I watch her whole body fall into the melody.

Then she starts to sing, and I fall into it too, her voice draws me in like it always has. She's in her element, so naturally talented. So fucking beautiful. I listen to the lyrics as she sings about tension, waiting, being afraid, and then when the chorus hits she's used my words. *Only Forever.*

The song is hauntingly beautiful, it builds, and she is completely immersed in it as she belts out the lyrics around the piano and I fall more and more as it continues. As she holds the last note, and it fades along with the sound from the piano the space feels even quieter than it did before she started.

"What do you think?" she asks, tucking a piece of hair behind her ear, her nervousness back.

"I – " I'm speechless, genuinely speechless. I can't form any words that would do it justice for what I want to tell her.

Instead of trying to find the right words I lean down, closing the short distance between us, take her face between my hands and press my mouth against hers.

5

SPENCER

I gasp against Jared's mouth before falling into the kiss. He's kissing me. Jared is *kissing me*. My brain catches up after my body. I'm reaching up, holding onto his thick forearms while his hands hold my face. His tongue teases the seam of my lips and I open for him to deepen the kiss.

Everything about this feels so different and so *right* between us. I was nervous to play that song for him. I poured so much of myself and my hidden feelings into it, the level of vulnerability is off the charts. But now he's kissing me, and I never want him to stop.

Our tongues are almost tentative in their exploration of each other, but none of this is uncomfortable. If anything, it's the most comfortable I've ever felt with another person. Eventually, after several minutes of our exploratory kisses he rests his forehead against mine.

"I planned for that to be a little smoother," he says with a breathy laugh.

I pull back to look at him better, his hands falling from my face to the side of my neck. I continue to hold onto his forearms because I feel like I need to keep physical contact with him. And if I don't he will disappear and I'll wake up from this dream.

"What do you mean?" I question.

"I just thought when I finally kissed you it would be softer, easing you into it. But listening to you sing. That song. I couldn't take it I just, *fuck* Spence," he drops his forehead back onto mine again and I smile.

"You just can't resist me, can you?" I tease. Our friendship has always been full of teasing and playful banter. Now that I feel like I can add flirtatious banter in there I am not holding back.

"You have no idea," he says softly before pressing his lips to mine once again.

I sigh against his mouth, already loving the feeling of kissing him and it's only the second time. I slide my hands up his forearms, then biceps, feeling the hard muscles along the way before standing and wrapping my arms around his back. I feel the ridges of muscles underneath my fingers and let out a quiet groan against his tongue. He moves his hands into my hair, tangling his fingers in the strands and angling my head how he likes.

What starts off as almost tentative, just learning each other's mouths turns heated quickly. Hands tighten, lips become harder and tongues rougher as we kiss and explore. Neither of us move our hands underneath clothing, but I'm tempted. I feel myself grow wetter from everything about the man in my arms, and I press myself harder against him to signal my want for more.

He pulls back again, breaking our kiss, and I can't stop the whimper I let out at the loss of contact.

"I don't want us moving too fast. I'm trying not to scare you off," he smiles.

I scoff. "You once filled my bathtub with frogs. You're not going to scare me off."

Laughing he says, "You've always hated frogs. That was hilarious though, you have to admit."

I put distance between us, keeping my hands on his hips, but removing my body from being plastered against his so he can see my narrowed eyes. "No. It wasn't. Those things are disgusting and you know what? I take it back, if you do that again then you *will* scare me off."

He just continues to laugh, yanking me against his body like he can't stand the space between us. "No more frogs, I promise."

With my body pressed against his again I feel the hardness in his pants pressing against my stomach. I bite back the joke about a snake I want to make because there's no denying what he has hidden behind his jeans is going to absolutely destroy me. And I can't wait.

WE SPEND the rest of the afternoon mostly innocent after deciding to try and diffuse some of the tension between us by watching some movies. It doesn't fully work because I continue to be turned on in his presence. Especially curled up on the couch next to him as his fingers trace the skin along my arm as he holds me against his side.

I run my hand along his thigh lightly, trying to tempt him, but it doesn't work. It's like he wants to torture us both to see how long we could possibly hold out before letting everything explode.

In reality, I think he's holding back in fear of being my rebound. So as much as I want to jump him, I can appreciate him being respectful. For now.

As the sun sets and our second movie ends, not that I've really been paying attention to anything other than where Jared is touching me, he speaks up, "I should probably head back for the night."

I groan in protest. "Just stay here."

Chuckling, he presses his lips to my forehead. "Can't do that, Superstar. We have rules that include sleeping in our hotel room the night before a game."

I bite my bottom lip to prevent myself from offering to *also* spend the night in his hotel room. He notices the look on my face and because he knows me so well, he's able to read the look easily.

"Not happening, Spence. I fucked up our first kiss, I refuse to do the same with anything else."

"You didn't fuck it up," I fold my arms across my chest. "It was perfect."

With a smile, he takes my face in his hands again to kiss me softly. I don't let it stay that way. Determined, I swing my leg over his lap to straddle him and push my tongue through his parted lips. He groans against me as I press down on him, rolling my hips feeling his quickly, hardening cock.

"Spencer," he growls against my lips before taking the bottom one between his teeth briefly.

"You could never be a rebound for me." I whisper in his ear, trailing my lips from his jaw, down his neck.

He lets me run my tongue across the skin of his neck, and I bite where it meets his shoulder which results in him grabbing my ass, pushing my body against his even harder. When my lips continue their journey up back to his lips, I kiss him deeply again. His hands slide up my back, up into my hair where they tangle against my scalp and then my head is yanked back by the strands. The bite of pain only makes my arousal kick up another notch. These panties are ruined, that's for damn sure.

"Listen to me," he growls, keeping his tight grip on my hair. "I want nothing more than to strip you down and plow into your perfect little cunt right here, but I'm not going to. Not yet. When I fuck you, Spencer, it's going to change both of our lives. It's going to mean you're mine. You're going to take my cock and as soon as you do there's no going back. Tell me you understand."

I gulp, I'm so fucking turned on. The demands. His growly

voice. The way he's tightly holding my hair, his dick hard and slightly rubbing against my pussy, only separated by a couple layers of flimsy fabric.

"Tell me," he demands again and I have to bite back a moan.

"I understand. When I take your cock then you're mine," I turn it around on him because it's true. If I'm going to be his, then he's going to be mine.

He chuckles darkly, running his lips along my throat, skimming his teeth up until he's speaking directly into my ear. "I'm already yours, I've just been waiting for you to catch up."

Fuck. He's not kidding about our lives changing once he fucks me because I'm pretty sure he's going to absolutely destroy me in more ways than one. And I've never wanted something so badly.

6

COLVER 30

It took every ounce of willpower I had to leave Spencer's house yesterday. I lingered at her door with our lips fused together while I seriously reconsidered the line in the sand I drew. I know this is for the best though. I need her to be sure about this. About us. And if we move too fast, there's the potential for her to regret it and I can't have that.

I wasn't even going to kiss her, but I couldn't stop myself after she sang that song for me. But I knew I wouldn't let it go further. The next time I have her alone, however, I don't think I'll be able to be so controlled.

Her body on mine, even clothed, I just know is going to be the end for me. I've known Spencer is it for me, I just accepted I would never fully have her and would have to settle for something less. Because everything is less compared to her.

But she's going to be mine and I wasn't kidding, it's going to change our lives. She doesn't know the extent I would go for her. She doesn't know how deep my feelings are already for her.

Another reason I'm trying to take it slow. I don't want to scare her with my full feelings right away.

Now, I'm in the locker room about to head out to the ice for our game against the L.A. Spartans. Which means having to see her piece of shit ex out there. I've never actually been in a fight during a game since being in the NHL. As a goalie we have less opportunities for them, generally if anything is close to starting my teammates are there. Everyone knows you don't touch the goalie in hockey.

It's going to take every thread of self-control I have to not beat that shit head Kenneth the second I see him.

∼

TURNS out *Kenneth* has it out for me as well apparently. He knows about me being friends with Spencer and I know he's always hated how much we talk. Now, it's like he knows there's more brewing between us. Or he's just an asshole who wants to fuck with me.

Every time he gets close to my net, he's spraying ice all over me, and there's been a couple times his stick has conveniently come into contact with my pads. Each sketchy move he makes has my teammates right there to push at him and put him in his place. It doesn't escalate, and he continues to say it was an accident.

Despite his shit, I'm on fire. Not a single puck has made it past me, and I intend to keep it that way. We have scored two goals and I'm prepping to make this a shutout. My first of the season.

It's the third period and I see guys heading my way, a Spartans player in possession of the puck. Of course, it's Kenneth and instead of him shooting it at a distance to give me a chance to stop it he continues barreling toward me, trying to get close and sneak it in. I push my stick out when he gets close, stopping him from turning at the last minute like he intended.

His skate collides with my stick, sending him flying right into me. Then all hell breaks loose.

"You fucking asshole," he screams before pushing me.

Fuck yeah. I can't help but be excited that he started it. My teammates descend on him, but I'm involved because I'm not letting them have all the fun. I throw my gloves down and start swinging my fists at him while he does the same. I'm more padded than he is so I barely feel his hits.

It's pandemonium in front of the goal as all the players that were on the ice are involved. Refs are whistling and trying to pull the group apart, but it's not working. Fists are flying from everyone on both teams with Kenneth and I in the middle of it all.

"You're the fucking asshole, did you just want to fuck with Spencer?" I spit at him with more punches.

"You don't know what you're talking about," he retorts.

"I know that you never deserved that woman."

He barks out a loud laugh, "And you do?"

"Fuck you," I swing at him, making contact with his face. I

faintly register my knuckles splitting, but I'm not going to stop.

Refs are continuing to break up the rest of the guys which takes quite a bit of effort and I'm being pulled away from Kenneth. Our helmets both came off at some point and I can see his smirk as he's skating backward, being pushed away by the ref. "Enjoy my sloppy seconds, Colver."

"Motherfucker," I go to charge after him again, but I'm held back.

"Bench," the ref says, and I snarl, skating to the bench where I know coach is going to pull me from the rest of the game. There isn't much left, and they ended up ejecting all the guys that were on the ice at the time for unsportsmanlike conduct.

Oh well. Worth it.

With the backup goalie in for me and five guys on each team out for the game we still manage to shut them out. My whole team is back in the locker room changing so we can get on the bus and back to the hotel. My teammate, McQuaid is next to me, and he asks, "What's the deal with you and Richardson?"

McQuaid was one of the guys on the ice that got kicked off with me, so he got to hear some of what went down between us. He was a little preoccupied in his own altercation so I wasn't sure how much he heard.

"Other than him being a fucking asshole," I mutter, throwing my jersey into my bag with a little more force than necessary.

McQuaid scoffs, "Yeah, we all know that. Did he make a move on your girl?"

"Not exactly. She's not my girl. *Yet.*"

"So? You want her, sounds like she's yours."

I laugh, of course that's his thinking. We aren't close, but I know McQuaid doesn't take "no" for an answer. He would understand my reason for hating Richardson.

"She was with Richardson for two years. But has been my best friend for the last twenty-four years."

"Isn't that like your whole life?"

"Pretty much. Turns out we've both wanted more and are just now realizing that, and I don't need her ex getting involved."

"Fuck yeah, man. Get your girl and kick that dude's ass. If you need help, I'm in."

"Thanks, but I think I got it handled," I shake my head. He's always down for a fight.

~

ON THE BUS back to the hotel I text Spencer. She was at the game up in the suite, but we didn't get to visit with anyone before leaving. I know a lot of the team is going out to celebrate the win. I highly doubt she wants to go anywhere. Going somewhere for her means paparazzi and fans. Which means no privacy. Okay, so maybe it's me being selfish with that and I want her alone.

I liked just being with her yesterday. Kissing her. Holding her. I'm not trying to rush it, even if my dick disagrees with that. Especially considering the fact that I had to jerk myself off while thinking about her as soon as I got back to the hotel yesterday.

> Jared: On the way back to the hotel. Want to hang out?

> Spencer: What hotel? I'll meet you there.

> Jared: You don't have to do that. I can come to you.

> Spencer: What hotel?

I shake my head at her persistence.

> Jared: Four Seasons.

> Spencer: Room?

> Jared: You don't have to come to my room. We can go out with the team or do anything you want.

> Spencer: Room.

I clench my phone tighter as my cock twitches. This may be a new thing we are exploring, but I know my best friend. I know when she's determined, and her mind is set on something. At this point I think I know what it is and I was sure we were going to wait a little longer.

But fuck who am I to argue if she has her mind made up.

7

SPENCER

I've been to more of Jared's games than I can count. He started playing hockey when we were really young, and I always liked going whenever his parents were willing to drag me along. However, I have never seen him get into a fight. I've seen him come close, but never actually come to blows like he did tonight. With my ex.

Even from the suite I was watching from, I could tell Kenneth was pulling some dirty shit out there. I wish I was surprised, but I'm not at all. And I know it was more than that for Jared to lose his shit like he did.

The result is that I've never been so turned on in my *life*.

I know he's trying to be sweet and gentlemanly, taking things slow. Make sure I'm *ready*. I can't help but mentally scoff at that. He doesn't know I've been checked out of my so-called relationship for almost a year before it actually ended.

We still had some good times, but they got fewer and

farther between. Now, I can't remember the last time I was truly happy with Kenneth. The one thing holding me back from full closure on that relationship, is that I have yet to scream at him for how he handled breaking up with me.

But that doesn't have anything to do with Jared and it really doesn't change the fact that he's not a rebound to me. He never could be.

That's why I'm on my way up to his hotel room, both nervous and excited for whatever is going to happen when I step through the door.

Brynn came with me to the game, but she's going to hang out with her brother, so she didn't mind me meeting up with Jared. In fact, she encouraged it as my friend. As my publicist she would rather I not be seen with another guy so soon. I told her that unless there's hidden cameras in his hotel room that isn't really a concern.

"Then go get the dick," were her parting words.

I make my way to the room number Jared told me he was in, and I can't help the anxiety trying to take over. Shaking my hands like it can shake away the lingering fear and dry them from the sweat that has started to appear. I finally raise my hand to knock.

It's like Jared was standing right on the other side waiting for me because the door swings open almost instantly. I take in his dark hair, still damp from his shower. He's removed his suit jacket and unbuttoned half of his shirt, showcasing the smooth muscled skin underneath. My eyes trail his body and the only thing I can think about is how it will feel. Finally, after all this time how it will feel on mine.

"Hey," he greets, and I don't even respond. I can't. I'm possessed in my need. The years of pent-up feelings and desires explode in a single moment.

So instead of saying anything in response, I barge forward, throwing my arms around his neck, yanking his lips down to mine in a scorching kiss. Instantly, his arms wrap around me, holding me tightly against his body while our mouths devour each other. He lifts me up and my legs wrap around his waist as he pulls me inside the room and shuts the door.

My back is slammed against the door he just closed at the same time his tongue rubs against mine in such a possessive way I moan into his mouth. Sliding my hands down his chest trying to undo the remainder of the buttons on his shirt. I growl in frustration against his lips, and he chuckles.

"Eager, Superstar?"

"Take off the shirt or I'm ripping it," I threaten.

He smiles, moving his mouth to my jaw, kissing all along it, down my neck, biting and sucking the skin as he goes.

"Fucking rip it then," he practically growls in my ear.

I moan at his words alone, tightening my legs around him to feel his erection pressed right against my core. Then I do what he says, taking the two sides of his shirt in my fists and ripping it so the buttons fly apart. His mouth doesn't leave mine as I work his shirt off his shoulders.

As I run my hands down the newly exposed skin, I groan at how amazing he feels. Hard muscles flexing under my exploring fingers. Then, I'm being lowered so my feet are back on the floor, and I protest with a whine and a nip at his bottom lip.

Jared pulls away from our kiss to give me an amused look. His hands remain on my waist and there's not an inch of space between us, but I liked being wrapped around him and this feels like he's slowing things down. Or stopping them completely which I'm definitely *not* okay with.

"I just want to look at you for a second," he says, his eyes scanning over my face and the top of my chest that isn't even exposed yet.

"Wouldn't you rather look at me while I'm naked?" I taunt, pulling at the hem of my shirt, but where his hands are resting prevent me from pulling it off.

"I just..." he shakes his head with a smile, "I can't believe this is happening. Are you sure?"

I roll my eyes. "Jared, I'm so serious when I say I don't think I've ever been more sure about anything in my life."

"I mean it. Once we do this, you're mine. You're my best friend and if you changed your mind and didn't want more, then I know I would lose all of you because I couldn't go back to just being your friend."

Neither could I. I know I couldn't see him with any other women after this. Or know what it feels like to touch him, kiss him, feel him inside me and pretend I don't. But I know one thing for sure.

"I'm not going to change my mind. So you better not either."

"Never."

His lips are on me once again, rough and demanding as he kisses me with so much passion, I feel lightheaded. He lifts my shirt up over my head and I quickly undo my bra because I just want to be naked with him already.

Once my chest is exposed, he pulls back again to look at me. I bite my bottom lip feeling the heat from his gaze on my skin.

"Fuck, this is what I've been missing?" he asks, pained.

"If you're already impressed then I'm going to blow your mind," I sass.

"You'll blow something alright, Superstar," he taunts, and I can't help but laugh. And to really surprise him I plan to do just that.

Dropping to my knees in front of him I yank at his pants, undoing the belt and opening them quickly.

"Wait," he stops my hands with his. "I didn't mean right now. I want to make you come first."

I look up at him through my lashes, "I just want a taste."

"*Fuck,* Spencer."

I smile, knowing I've won. I shake his hands off mine to continue to work at his pants, yanking them down, revealing his boxers and the large bulge in them. I grope him through the fabric resulting in a hiss from his lips.

My hands grip the waistband of his boxers where I trace the skin slightly before pulling them down to reveal his thick and very hard cock that is pointing right at me. I swipe my tongue over my bottom lip just taking him in before wrapping my hand around his thickness. I'm going to struggle to take him in any part of me. But I like a challenge.

"Spencer," he moans from above me, almost pained as I stroke him once.

"Yeah?" I ask, with another stroke.

"If you don't put me in your mouth in the next two seconds, I'm going to lose my shit."

I flick my tongue over the head of his dick, swiping the bead of precum there and he groans loudly. I love when men make noise, I want to hear more of it. Which is why instead of teasing him more like I want to, I wrap my lips around him and try to take him into the back of my throat.

"Holy shit," he moans above me. I smile around him, pulling back slightly to attempt and get more.

I pull off him for a moment, but keep my grip, moving my hand up and down slowly. "I don't think I've ever seen anything as sexy as you fighting with my asshole ex."

He quickly collars his hand around my throat, forcing me to look up at him. "Don't you ever mention anyone else while you have my cock in your hand."

I refuse to admit how the single sentence has my panties completely flooded.

"I'm just saying I don't think I've ever been as turned on as I was watching you."

"Show me."

I reach into my pants, swiping through the wetness and bringing my glistening fingers up to show him.

Removing his hand from my throat, which I want to demand back, he takes my fingers into his mouth and sucks them clean. I whimper at the movement and as soon as he frees my hand from his grasp, I'm back to taking him all into my mouth.

His hands slide through my hair, gripping the strands tightly. I can tell he's holding back from using me how he wants. I continue my efforts to take all of him in my throat, but I'm not that talented apparently. Using my hand on the part of him I can't fit, I bob my head while suctioning which only makes him moan louder.

"Spence," he grits through clenched teeth while his hands tighten in my hair.

I take him farther than I have this entire time, but I'm ripped off by my hair and he yanks me back up to standing, crushing his mouth to mine. This kiss is messy and primal and fucking *everything*.

He picks me up again, but this time he carries me to the bed, throwing me down. I bounce as soon as my back hits the mattress. I look up at him, still standing at the end of it. A thin sheen of sweat covers his heaving chest, dick standing straight up that looks seconds away from exploding.

I lean up on my elbows as he quickly undoes my jeans and pulls them off me roughly, taking my panties along with it.

"Last chance to end this. Once I fuck you, you're mine."

"I already am."

He's on me before I can even finish the last word. Lips on mine, tongue, teeth, everything pulling gasps and moans from me as he rubs his thick cock against my soaking slit. I'm already so close I feel like I could explode, but he reaches down and starts circling my clit with his fingers.

I cry out at the sensation as his mouth travels across my chest, down my neck and to my breasts, licking one of my nipples before sucking it into his mouth the moment his finger plunges inside me.

"Fuck, Jared, I want more please," I cry out. It feels good, but I'm impatient and want him to fuck me.

He bites the spot where my neck meets my shoulder, "Shut the fuck up and take what I give you," he growls against my skin the same time he pushes another finger inside me.

I gasp, my eyes rolling back in my head from both his words and the sensations his hands are causing within me. He's never spoken to me like that before. I've never heard him say anything like that at all. But I've also never been in bed about to be fucked within an inch of my life by him either.

Oh my god, I'm about to fuck Jared. Jared Colver. My best friend. The boy turned man who I've wanted, but never thought I could ever have.

"Are you going to come for me? Show me how badly you've wanted me for years?" His voice is low and husky against my ear.

I can't speak, so I nod my head like a crazed maniac. Probably because that's exactly what I'm feeling like as I feel the telltale signs of release building quickly. Especially when he pumps his fingers harder, curling them perfectly which sends me straight to an orgasm that has me gasping and writhing underneath him.

As I come back down to earth, my vision returns as I open my eyes. I'm greeted with Jared's sexy as sin face looming above me and looking at me like he's just witnessed something magical.

"What?" I giggle, squirming around in his hold. He quickly slides one of his legs between mine, his thigh grazing my sensitive clit resulting in another startled gasp from my throat.

"I've always thought you were beautiful when you sing. But that is now my second favorite sound that comes out of this mouth. The sounds you make when you come are the first. Hands down."

"Guess that means it's my turn to hear what you sound like when *you* come," I run my hand down his hard chest to his even harder erection resting against me. "Fuck me, Jared. I want to feel you."

"You want my cock, Superstar?" His teeth bite my bottom lip before sucking it into his mouth.

I think I moan out a weak *yes*, but it's lost in Jared's mouth as he kisses me with so much heat and passion I'm rutting against him, trying to get him inside me.

"Say it. Tell me how much you want it. Beg me for it," he commands.

"*Please,* Jared. I want your cock. I want you. *Please.*"

"Alright, alright, if you insist," he chuckles, adjusting his hips in between my legs, lining himself up with my entrance. He knows I'm on birth control and that we are both clean, so I don't bother to bring up a condom. I wouldn't want him to wear one anyway. I want to feel him.

"Oh my god, you're so anno – " he cuts me off with his mouth on mine and the snap of his hips, pushing inside me with a solid thrust that has me crying out into his mouth.

Jared groans, dropping his head to my shoulder, rocking his hips back slightly before pushing back in as far as he can go.

"You feel too good, *fuck* Spencer, how can you feel this good?"

"You feel fucking *huge*," is all I'm able to say because he does. I feel myself stretched around him, painful but in the best way.

"Are you okay?" he asks, softly, a stark contrast to how he has been up until this point. It's then I realize how tense I am as I adjust to his size and to the realization that this is really happening between us.

"Yes, yeah, so good. Please move, Jared," I buck my hips up trying to get him to move. Attempting to get him impossibly deeper.

He does what I want and moves. Pulling his hips back, almost completely pulling out before thrusting forward again, hard. I practically scream, trying to muffle it in his chest. He loses all control he may have had up until this point. Taking one of my legs over his shoulder, then bending the other so it's around his waist he fucks me. Hard thrusts, impaling me over and over in a way that has me breathless.

The angle of his hips has him rubbing me in the best way from the inside, while his pelvis hits my clit with every thrust. I'm barreling toward another release, one that I know will be stronger than the first.

"Why the fuck did we wait so long to do this?" he grunts.

All I can do is moan because I'm completely lost in the sensation of *him*. Of what we are doing and how amazing it feels. I never want it to end. I just want to continue to be lost in this. In *him* for the rest of my life.

It doesn't take long before I'm crying out in ecstasy once

again, my nails digging into his back just trying to hold onto something as I fall deeper and deeper into my orgasm. His thrusts grow choppy as he chases his own and then he's pulsing inside of me, which only triggers aftershocks of my own.

Jared's movements slow, but he stays in place as we both come down. He's pressing soft kisses along my collarbone, up my neck until he gets to my mouth. We kiss softly, slowly, just feeling each other.

Eventually our kisses stop, and he pulls back to look at me, eyes shining even in the dark. I can't imagine how crazy I must look with thoroughly fucked makeup and hair. None of that matters with the way he's looking at me, though. Because what I see in his eyes is admiration and satisfaction.

"Wow," he breathes, and I can't help but chuckle.

"Was it everything you dreamed it would be?"

"Better," he nuzzles into my neck, "I don't know how it's possible, but so much better."

8

COLVER 30

We lay in bed; Spencer curled against my side. My arm is wrapped around her as I run my fingers along her arm. We are both still naked and it doesn't seem like we want to change that any time soon.

I can't believe this is really happening. Spencer and me. *Finally*. Fuck, she's amazing.

"I have to be honest about something," she says, breaking the comfortable silence we've found ourselves in.

"Hm?" I hum, and normally I think those words would make me nervous, but frankly I'm so relaxed and spent that I can't even bring myself to be worried.

"I've actually seen you naked before tonight," she turns into my chest with soft laughter.

I pull away slightly to look at her, seeing the humor reflected on her face, but I'm just confused. "When?"

"A couple years ago, when we went to that lake house. I had just started dating..." her voice trails off and I tense, really not wanting to hear his name while we are naked and wrapped around each other. "You know who," she finishes.

I huff, still not pleased with the reminder that she was with someone, let alone someone so shitty for so long.

"I felt bad at the time," she adds softly. "Because I was so tempted to touch you that day."

"When did you see me naked?" I ask, unable to place any time that would have been possible.

She smiles, remembering the moment she's referring to, "We all just got done from going on the boat and swimming. Everyone claimed a shower, you opted for the one outside. I walked by as you were...preparing to get into it."

That specific memory doesn't stick out as anything important to me because it was just a basic shower since I didn't know Spencer saw me. Maybe if I did, things would have been a bit different. Even if she had a boyfriend, it may not have stopped me. Especially since I've never liked him.

"I wish I knew you saw me then," I tell her.

"Why's that?"

"Because I bet you stared a bit too long. Made you wet." I give her a look, waiting for her to confirm what I'm assuming.

"Maybe."

"Then, if I caught you, and *fuck* I wish I did, I would have stripped you down and had you join me in that cold shower. We could have heated it up."

She bites at her bottom lip, thinking, "I wouldn't have stopped you."

Maybe it's terrible to be glad she would've given in, boyfriend or not. I think it was going to be us no matter what. At some point in our lives, it was always going to be us. Just like this.

I can't help it, I roll over, trapping her underneath my body weight. My dick already hard and ready for her again, rubbing against her thigh.

"So, that means you won't stop me now?" I ask with a raised eyebrow.

"I don't think it's *possible* for me to stop you."

I give her a wicked smile, "Good."

Then I'm sliding lower, kissing down her naked body until I'm in between her legs and face to face with her addicting pussy. She's wet with a mix of our releases and it's so fucking hot to see that I'm losing my mind. I lean forward giving a long lick up her entire slit.

She gasps, yanking my hair and pulling my head up to look at her, remaining between her legs. "You don't have to do that because you...you know."

"Because I came in you?"

She bites her bottom lip with a nod.

"Spencer, I don't give a fuck. We taste amazing together and I'm going to make you come on my tongue before you come on my cock again."

Her mouth drops open on a gasp that turns into a moan when I latch my mouth on her clit and suck. Pushing two fingers inside her swollen pussy I pump slowly while flicking my tongue against her bundle of nerves until she's moaning loudly. I know she's getting close again.

I alternate between sucking and flicking, finding the perfect rhythm that has her writhing underneath me all while pumping my fingers. She's yanking at my hair, bucking her hips up, trying to do everything to find the release I'm so desperate to give her.

I moan against her cunt, sending a vibration through her that has her crying out in pleasure as she clamps down on my fingers. I continue my assault on her clit to pull every ounce of her orgasm out of her.

She's chanting my name, and a chorus of other cuss words and *oh God*. I have never felt more powerful than I do at this moment. Sure, I've been with other women, usually quick hookups I don't care to put much effort in. Spencer is different. I want to take my time. I want to do everything with her just to see her reaction. I want her noises, her looks, her feelings. Her *everything*.

Spencer yanks me up her body once her orgasm has subsided and kisses me fiercely. She licks at my mouth like she wants the taste of both of us in her mouth as well, and I let her. When she tries to lift up her hips to have me push inside her again, I pull my mouth away from hers to flip her onto her stomach.

My hands grip her hips tightly, pulling her up onto her knees before pushing inside her tight wet heat again. She drops her head onto the mattress, moaning as her hands grip the sheets tightly.

"Fuck, Jared, how are you *deeper*?" She pushes back against me, so her ass is slapping against my skin.

I lean forward to drape over her back and speak directly into her ear as I give her shallow thrusts to keep the friction between us. "I want to be as deep as possible in you, I want you to feel me for days and remember tonight. I want to be so ingrained in your body and your mind that you can't do a single thing without thinking about me. I want you as distracted and obsessed with me as I am with you, Spencer."

"I already am," she whispers.

I take her hands in mine, locking our fingers together and pushing them forward so she's completely flat on her stomach underneath me as I pound into her. I continue to hold her hands hostage. She squeezes my fingers tightly with hers as her moans are muffled into the mattress and I fuck her into it.

"Come for me again," I demand because I'm so close and I

need her to let go first. "I know you're close, I can feel you squeezing my cock. Let go."

And she does. Her pussy is a vice around me as she comes and it sends me over the edge once again, releasing inside her. Maybe we should've used condoms, but I didn't want there to be anything between us. If she had said anything, I would have worn one, but she didn't so I assume she feels a similar way.

I roll off her back, pulling her into me so she's laying on my chest again. I like the feel of her there, her head resting against my heart, her hand running along my skin. Her touch is light until she decides to scratch slightly.

"When do you have to leave?" Her voice is soft, and I can hear how tired she is.

I grimace at the reminder, pressing my lips against her hair as I answer, "In the morning."

"That's okay, I have a couple shows in Texas this next week."

I smile knowingly because I'm planning on attending the one in Dallas. The only one that I'm able to since we have a small break in the schedule. I'll have to leave right after morning skate that day, but I'll be able to make it. She doesn't look up to see my reaction and I feel her breathing even out signaling she's asleep.

I expected her to say a bit more about the fight I got in earlier, but I'm a little surprised she didn't. Instead, practically attacking me the second she walked in the door. That, plus showing me how much it turned her on. I can safely say that's a good sign, but I have a feeling this whole ex situation isn't over quite yet. Even my fight with him felt unfinished.

One thing that won't change, no matter what, is that Spencer is officially mine.

9

SPENCER

I vaguely remember lips kissing me awake and Jared's voice telling me he has to leave. I think I reached for him and attempted to pull him back into the bed with me. I'm pretty sure he laughed while breaking free of my grasp that was weak with exhaustion. It didn't take long until I was asleep again because I don't even remember the door closing.

By the time I wake up, the space on the bed where Jared was is cold. I don't know what time he left, but it must have been early. My body is sore with the reminder of what we did last night. I hate that we have to be apart now for I don't know how long. Maybe this was a stupid thing to do while he's in the middle of his season and I'm on a tour.

On the other hand, I don't want to waste any more time with us battling our feelings for each other. It isn't fair. Part of me hates myself even more for staying with Kenneth as long as I did when that was a big roadblock from anything happening with Jared.

Ugh. Speaking of Kenneth, I saw he tried calling me last night. Plus, the several texts from him that have remained unread. I want to ignore his entire presence and forget that he ever existed. Erase him completely from my life as if he was never there.

Unfortunately, that's not possible and I need to talk to Brynn about how to handle this moving forward. We've kept a low profile these last couple weeks because she said right now it is best to not address anything and let it blow over.

I'm done with that plan, though. I want to put it to rest because the last thing I need is any press coming out about Jared and me to then start the rumor mill about me cheating. I'm sure that's exactly what Kenneth wants. He would love nothing more than to ruin my image if he's no longer benefiting from it. But that will never happen.

∽

Brynn comes over to my house that afternoon. After I managed to pull myself from the hotel bed and go home, I took the longest shower in history. The warm water soothed my aching muscles from being so perfectly overworked last night.

Jared texted me when he got back home and it's ridiculous how much I already miss him. Especially considering we've been long distance friends for so long, it's like he's not anywhere near me anymore and my body knows it. And doesn't like it.

"Tell me everything," Brynn starts when she comes into my house. "After that fight for your honor, I know it had to be good."

I laugh. "You don't need the gory details," I pause, "but yeah, it was good."

"I knew it! You two have always had this crazy chemistry. Of course it's amazing once you finally let it all out."

I wave her off, "Enough about that. How was seeing your brother?"

"That's a boring topic. It was fine. Brent is Brent, annoying older brother. Oh, he was not happy when we were leaving, and Kenneth's teammate tried talking to me."

I tilt my head, "Which one?"

"The annoying one that always tries to talk to me. Tall, light brown hair, kind of a dick."

I bust out a laugh, "That's like half the team."

"That one, fuck, what is his name?" she shakes her head, thinking. "Cole?"

I try to think about the team roster and there's not a Cole on the team. "Oh, Colton?"

"Yeah, that one."

"He is kind of a dick," I agree, scrunching my face. Kenneth is number one asshole, but Colton might be a close second. He has tried to talk to Brynn on a few occasions when we've been to games, but she isn't interested at all. Hockey guys are a giant no for her because of who her brother is.

"Anyway, enough about that. Let's deal with what you pay me for."

"Right, what should we do? He can't have the last word about this, and he can't make me look like the bad guy."

"Have you talked to him at all?"

"Nope. He's reached out, but I haven't even opened the texts."

"Let's start there. I'm curious what he's saying." She stretches out her hand for me to give her my phone. I appreciate her knowing I don't want to see the texts and that she can handle it.

I lay back on my couch taking inventory on my sore body, deciding later I'm going to take a lavender Epsom salt bath. Maybe I'll FaceTime with Jared while I'm in said bath. *Hm now that's an idea.*

I'm humming a new melody, drumming my fingers like I'm playing the song on a piano. It's like my mind has exploded with song ideas after last night. I could probably create an entire album based just on those eight hours I spent wrapped up in Jared.

"He's such an idiot," Brynn says, pulling me out of my thoughts.

"Why? I mean yes, but why?"

She shakes her head, locking my phone and setting it down.

"He wants to meet up to talk to you, claims he wants to explain and that it isn't what it seems."

I can tell she's not telling me everything and I narrow my eyes at her, "What else?"

"There were some comments about sicking your guard dog on him."

I can't help the laugh that bursts out of me. "What an idiot. I would hardly call Jared my guard dog, but even if he was, I know that if I had it my way he would've done a lot more damage."

"Maybe when their teams play each other again you can see about having that arranged," she winks.

"I just might," I chuckle. "So, how are we going to handle this shit because I would rather be done."

I watch as Brynn gets into her publicist mode, "Okay, you're not going to like it at first."

I groan, "What?"

"You should talk to him. Privately. See if you can come to a mutual agreement on this, then each of you can issue an identical statement."

"Mhm," I look at her skeptically. "And when he tells me to take my mutual agreement and shove it up my ass. Then what?"

"Then, we go with plan B and try to be cordial in a statement while trying to preserve your image."

"Right. And then I release all the scathing songs I've written about him and ride off into the sunset with a sexy goalie on a rival team."

"As long as you don't say his name in the songs, I don't have a problem with that."

"Good because I'm doing that regardless."

∽

As I suspected, Kenneth has not agreed to meet with me. At least that's my assumption since he hasn't replied at all to the text Brynn sent from my phone asking. I'm pretty sure he's just being petty and ignoring me like I ignored him for a while.

Oh well, he's not the one who has been on my mind anyway. Jared and I have continued to talk constantly, but our once innocent conversations now have a flirty and sexual edge to them. The worst part of this is not being able to see him as often as I would like. It hasn't even been a week and I'm dying for him again which is only made worse by the fact that I have no idea when I'll get to see him.

I'm on the plane heading to Dallas for my next show tomorrow night. My whole team including the band are here as well, but my manager, Laura, is going over my schedule with me.

"And after the show tomorrow you have an interview set up," she explains.

"*After?* No, I don't do press after shows. I'm too tired, sweaty, and gross."

"It's not a visual interview and this is the only time you have."

I scrunch my face, still not happy with the idea. I barely want to talk to people I like to be around after a show, let alone do an interview. "Ten minutes max, then I get to go back to the hotel for the night."

"That's fine," she agrees and I'm a little surprised. Laura isn't a hard ass per se, but I can admittedly be a little difficult when it comes to certain press tasks, so she and Brynn tend to have their work cut out for them.

I love what I do. I love performing and meeting fans. I just don't love talking about myself in interviews. I do my sharing about who I am through my music, and I just wish that could be enough. Of course, every interviewer is provided with a "don't ask" list for my hard no topics.

Though, there has been a time or two when that list has been ignored which leads to an extremely awkward time for both me and them.

Once we land, I text Jared just like I told him I would.

> Spencer: Just landed in Dallas. Wish you were here with me.

> Jared: Me too, Superstar. Maybe you should only tour in the off season so I can be with you the entire time.

> Spencer: I'll be making that my tour stipulation from now on.

10

COLVER 30

After morning skate, I drove straight to the airport and got on a direct flight from Denver to Dallas. I talked to Brynn and got the information for her manager Laura to set up a fake interview to surprise her after the show. I got the rest of the information I needed from Brynn including the hotel she will be staying at and when it's safe for me to stop by so she won't be there before the show.

It's all very elaborate because I don't do half ass surprises, I go all out for those I care about. Plus, I love the look on her face when she's surprised.

She texted me that she landed when I just got to the airport for my own flight. Once I land, I know she's already at the venue getting ready, doing sound check and everything else she has to do. So, I take an Uber to the hotel to shower and change.

I have a spot in the designated VIP section of the stadium. Brynn sent me everything I'll need to get in and assured me that Spencer wouldn't see or know I'm here. As the concert starts, her opening act performs and I hadn't heard of the band before, but they were pretty good. Definitely a rock group which doesn't surprise me because my girl loves rock.

Once they are done there's a short break before the lights in the stadium cut out completely and a guitar starts a powerful riff. Bass and drums join in so strong the floor is actually vibrating underneath my feet. Then, I hear her, the voice that consumes almost every thought I have. The slight rasp she has when she hits certain notes, but the overall power when she sings gives me chills.

She appears on stage, her auburn hair almost a glowing halo under the spotlights as she belts out one of her more popular songs. I love every angle of Spencer. When I have her alone, when she's in her element up there performing for thousands. Everything about her is intoxicating to me. I've always known I love her. She's my best friend, of course I love her.

But fuck I *love* her.

Maybe it's ridiculous to think since we are just now exploring a different type of relationship, but I think I've felt this type of love for her for a while and just never accepted it, not knowing if she's mine. But now she is and there's nothing that can hold back the emotion that has exploded in my chest.

She continues to perform and just like Brynn said I don't think she's seen me. I'm completely entranced by her. I've seen her perform before, many times, but it never ceases to amaze me.

About halfway through her set she sits down at a piano on the stage and speaks into the microphone attached to it.

"I have a new song I want to play for you all tonight. This is a song I wrote recently," she looks down and I see the grin she sports even through the curtain of her hair that hides most of her face. "It's pretty special to me. It's about having feelings for someone, but you aren't sure if they feel the same."

I instantly recognize the song as soon as her fingers move over the keyboard. It's the one she sang for me at her house. The one she wrote for *me*. I'm lost in everything about it, everything about her as she sings. It was good when she played it for me before but hearing it taking over this giant stadium makes it even more powerful.

The audience loses it as soon as she finishes.

Chuckling into the microphone, "Safe to say you guys like it, then?"

The screams increase and I watch Spencer smile so wide, clearly so happy everyone loves the song. She continues the concert and as much as I'm enjoying it, I can't wait to have her alone again. I need to have my hands on her. My tongue. My cock. *Fuck* I'm going to have to hide a boner walking out of this place because now I can't stop thinking of exactly what I'm going do to her as soon as I see her.

∼

I CAME backstage during her last song. Even though I would have loved to watch her finale, I want to surprise her more. I was brought into her dressing room so I can sit in one of the chairs and wait for her.

Luckily, I'm able to hear her singing the loud and powerful song that is about getting over someone. I'm trying to think about who this one could be about, but I know sometimes she writes songs just for fun and fake scenarios. She has the perfect balance of songs about life experiences and ones she makes up.

As soon as the song is over, I hear her announce for the audience to clap for her band, backup singers, dancers, and the whole production team. The cheers are loud even in here, but out there it's deafening.

I straighten in the chair because she will be back here any minute. I feel like a teenager, or some shit all giddy to see my crush. I know what that feels like since I *am* about to see my teenage crush. But we are adults now which means we don't have to sneak around, and thank God. I would combust if I had to navigate sneaking around parents or friends to be able to touch her. I'm a man possessed for this woman and I'm not even ashamed.

After a few more minutes I finally hear voices from outside the door, they start out quiet and get louder, so I know they are approaching.

"Can you please cancel it?" Spencer asks someone.

"No can do, just get freshened up. It won't take very long," Brynn encourages, and I smile. They are close.

"I'm starting to feel sick," Spencer lets out the fakest cough.

"Just make yourself pretty again, then I promise it'll be okay."

Spencer is groaning when she practically falls into the room dramatically.

"Hey Superstar," I greet, which makes her immediately stand up straight with a shocked look.

Her face quickly transforms into excitement when she realizes it's me, then she launches herself at me. I barely get to stand before she's wrapping her arms and legs around my body. I can't help the chuckle I let out into her neck right before she yanks my face to hers in a deep kiss.

I almost forget we aren't entirely alone as our kiss borderlines inappropriate when Spencer rolls her hips against me and moans against my tongue that is currently caressing hers as my hands yank at her sweat soaked hair.

Somehow, she pulls back just slightly to speak to whoever is nearby, "You better cancel that fucking interview because I'm definitely not going now."

I breathe out a laugh right before her lips are back on mine, both of us searching, and so hungry for each other nothing else matters.

"Spencer, this is your interview," someone, I think Brynn, answers. Frankly, I'm too wrapped up in the woman who is hanging onto me like a koala to think about who is around right now.

Spencer pulls back from my mouth again, and I try to chase

after her, but she doesn't let me with a grip on my hair. "If this is my interview, I expect a raving article about how amazing I am," she teases.

I huff out a laugh against her lips. "Baby, you'll get all positive reviews from me, you know that. Five stars all around." I drop my voice so only she can hear me. "Five star fucking pussy that I can't wait to make mine again."

She moans quietly, "You're going to have to fuck me here because I don't think I'll be able to wait until the hotel."

I kiss her once again, but don't let her deepen it when she tries to. Instead, I pull back and slide her body down mine, despite her reluctance and the cute pissed off look she has on her face.

"The things I'm planning to do to you can't be done here. Even doing them at the hotel is pushing it because we might end up getting kicked out from your screams."

She scoffs and I see the challenge in her eyes. "Guarantee you'll be louder. You're not very quiet, you know?"

"Oh, I'm very aware. I want you to hear me, but trust me, Superstar, you're going to scream my name for the rest of the night. So, let's get out of here."

I start to walk toward the door, but she quickly stops me with a hand on my forearm. "Why are you leaving?"

"Because I know for a damn fact if you get naked right now, you'll convince me to fuck you and I already told you that's not happening here."

"Your self control is actually disgusting, you know that?"

I shake my head with a laugh. "I'm hanging on by a thread. And trust me, when we get back, you'll see."

"Can't wait."

11

SPENCER

Thank *God* my interview wasn't really an interview and is actually a dick appointment with Jared. I was seconds away from running and hiding somewhere until I could escape the interview before I saw him.

Also, yes, I have in fact done that before and I'm not proud of it. Sometimes you do what you have to do. But I don't make that a habit.

I changed as fast as I possibly could, and let my crew grab my things. Normally I pack up, but I'm too keyed up to waste any more time. I've missed Jared too much; I know I don't have a lot of time with him tonight so I'm about to take advantage of every second I have.

My driver takes us back to the hotel and despite my attempted advances in the car, he's apparently standing his ground because he took my hand in his own, kissed my palm and intertwined our fingers.

"You're trying to kill me. Death by blue balls," I tell him.

He throws his head back with laughter, "Since when do you have balls?"

"Since you've insisted on making them blue and killing me with them."

"I promise, if I'm going to kill you with anything it would be with orgasms," he kisses the back of my hand.

"Well, you're not doing a very good job of that right now," I huff.

With a raised eyebrow, he looks me up and down but doesn't say anything. I feel like my skin is on fire just from the look alone. This new side of Jared is so much more than I ever expected. He's always so nice to me, so sweet and sensitive. I figured sex with him would be the same. I was clearly very wrong, and I have a feeling tonight I'm going to see even more of this new side. That's probably why I continue to try and press his buttons because I know the more I can rile him up, the more I'll reap the rewards.

He stays eerily calm as we arrive at the hotel and get into the elevator. I want him to attack me as soon as the doors slide closed. I want his mouth on mine again, biting and licking and to not let go even while we stumble to my room.

That's not what happens. The doors shut and I suck in a breath in anticipation, but he doesn't move. My hand remains in his and he doesn't yank me against his body. He doesn't push me against the wall. He doesn't even *say* anything. It's starting to piss me off. I'm wondering if I even imagined everything that's happened between us because at this moment, he doesn't seem like someone who's ready to rip my clothes off.

We get to the door; he pulls out a key card and opens it for us.

"How did you get a key to my room?" I ask, breaking the silence between us.

He still doesn't say anything, though. Just looks back at me, winks and pulls me into the room. He continues to say nothing as he leads me into the bedroom of the suite. He has me stand at the end of the bed before stepping back and leaning against the wall across from me. I'm breathing hard in anticipation. I have no idea what he plans to do right now, but I want it. I want all of it.

"Strip," he commands. One word. One simple word and I'm already a puddle at his feet.

I think I blackout or hallucinate, but either way I don't act fast enough for Jared, apparently.

"Take off your clothes, Spencer. Show me what's mine."

Fuck.

"You – " I stutter while starting to take off the t-shirt and jeans I changed into at the venue. "You can't say things like that."

"Oh, I can't? Why?"

"Because I'm pretty sure I'll pass out from how sexy it is."

"Thought I was giving you blue balls."

I finally wrestle out of my jeans, leaving me completely naked, standing in a hotel room a few feet from my childhood best friend turned man who I want to fuck me into next week.

"You still are since you're over there fully clothed," I gesture down his body.

"Get on the bed and show me that pussy," he instructs, ignoring what I said.

I want to sass him, but I want him to touch me more, so I do what he says. Sitting on the foot of the bed I bring my feet up to rest on the mattress, spreading myself wide for him to see. And I know he's seeing how wet I already am, between the dressing room, the anticipation, the growly way he's commanding me now. I'm *soaked*.

"Fuck, Spence, do you know how beautiful you are? How absolutely perfect? I want to spend the rest of my life buried in that dripping cunt. So fucking wet for me."

I moan and can't help but slide my hand around to touch myself, if he's not going to then I will. I hardly swipe my fingers over my clit before he's storming across the room to me, slapping my hand away and pinning my wrists to the bed, leaning over me. I whimper at the loss but stare up at him.

"I didn't tell you to touch. *I* make you come. Got it?"

My bottom lip is trapped between my teeth with a nod.

"Good. Does your throat hurt from your show tonight?"

I shake my head. The voice is like any other muscle and gets stronger when it is worked. It's been a while since I've been hoarse or had a sore throat after performing.

"Then it won't be a problem for you to scream so loud everyone in this hotel knows what I'm doing to you," he says with a wink before dipping his head down and licking my pussy from top to bottom.

I let out a gasp at the feeling of his warm wet tongue on me, providing the perfect pressure but only for a moment. I wiggle my hips trying to get his mouth back on me.

"Not loud enough, Spencer, I expect better from you."

He does it again, this time suctions my clit *hard*.

"Oh my god!" I cry out, and not just because he told me to.

"That's better. But I want *my* name on those perfect lips."

He lets go of my wrists to hold onto my thighs, pushing them wide before his mouth is back on me, this time he licks, sucks, and then plunges his tongue inside. My hands grip his hair holding him to me while my hips buck up against him and a cry of his name is on my lips.

It's so much, it's not enough. It's everything I want and yet I also want more. I'm held open by his strong hands while he feasts on me, and I don't think I've ever felt so frantic for anything than I am for my orgasm. He keeps teasing it out of me with strong suctions and flicks of his tongue, but then pulls back and teases me with softer licks everywhere except where I want him to be.

"Jared, please stop fucking teasing me," I moan, yanking at his hair to try and keep him giving me the exact pressure that will make me see stars, but he manages to lighten back up.

He makes some noise against me, and the vibration almost has me there, but it's still not quite enough and I groan in frustration.

His hand comes down on my pussy, hard.

I gasp, sitting up on my elbows. "Did you just spank my pussy?"

"Fuck. Say pussy again."

"Pussy," I tease.

"Yes, I did. And I can tell that you liked it so I'm going to do it again and again until your *cunt* comes for me. How about that?" He ends his sentence with another sharp smack that has me moaning. "Tell me, Spencer. Do you like having your pussy slapped?"

His palm meets my flesh again. I cry out. I'm so close just from this, I never would have expected it. How am I this close from being fucking *slapped*?

"Words, Superstar."

Slap.

"Yes, *Ah, yes,* Jared. I like it. I'm so close. Oh *fuck.*"

It's like something breaks loose in him from hearing me admit it. He slaps me again before returning to licking and sucking this time he doesn't let up. The orgasm is building and building so fast I couldn't stop it even if he wanted me to or if I tried. I'm going to fall over the edge so hard and I know that's exactly what he wants.

When I explode, I scream his name, curses and other things I'm not even sure make sense because all I know is the blinding pleasure rushing through my body. I think I hear him telling me how good I am, and how amazing I look, but I can barely hear any of it until the euphoric feeling subsides enough for me to regain my senses.

He's looking up at me, the bottom half of his face wet with my release. He licks his lips obscenely and it only makes me want every part of him to be touching every part of me.

"That was so fucking beautiful, Spence. *You* are so fucking beautiful."

I don't have the capacity to come up with any witty thing to say like I want to. Instead, I yank at his hair to signal that I want him. He follows my lead, letting me pull him up my body so I can lick at his mouth, tasting myself on his lips before he plunges his tongue into my mouth, overwhelming me with the taste of both my cum and just *him*.

When he starts trailing open mouth kisses along my jaw and my neck I attempt to speak, "I've never...that..." My voice trails off on another moan as he moves lower and sucks my nipple into his mouth, grazing his teeth over the hard point.

"I know, baby," he says around my breast before trailing over to the other one and doing the same thing on that side.

It's this moment when my sensitive skin is being grazed by fabric, I remember he's still *very* clothed. And I need his skin touching mine. I need him on me. In me. I need to be surrounded and lost in Jared Colver. Reaching down, I pull at his shirt to try to rip it off, or just plain rip it. I'd honestly be fine with either.

He knows what I'm doing and pulls on my nipple, pulling it slightly before letting it go roughly. He moves to stand at the end of the bed, reaching behind his back to pull off his shirt first, then moving to undo his pants, and push them down. He keeps his boxers on, and when he tries to climb back over me, I plant my foot on his thigh, stopping him.

"Naked, Colver," I say, finally able to use my words again. But just barely.

He smiles, "Whatever you want, Superstar."

Pushing down his boxers, his cock bobs free. So hard, so long and thick and intimidating. I don't think it matters how many times I fuck this man; I'll continue to wonder how he is able to fit inside me without splitting me in half.

"I can see you thinking. What is it?" he asks with an amused look while running his hand over his length, pumping slowly while his eyes stay locked on mine.

I smirk up at him, not wanting to share where my thoughts really were. "Just wondering if you're going to stand there staring or if you're actually going to fuck me. Unless you're scared?"

His eyebrows shoot up. "Scared?"

"Mhm. I know how intimidating I am. Especially for you, and I get having a little bit of stage fright." I'm totally kidding. One hundred percent kidding which I'm somehow able to joke while he's not touching me because I short circuit the second his hands are on me.

"You think I have stage fright about fucking you?" I think he can tell I'm kidding. He's always been able to read me.

"Yup, it's okay. We can figure it out, I'm sure. There's pills you can – " he cuts me off by grabbing my ankles and flipping me onto my stomach. I gasp at the sudden movement and before I can even attempt to flip back over, he's on me, pressing his weight onto my back. His erection is pressed between my legs. If he moves, he will give me some friction I'm craving, but with how tightly pressed together my legs are, he's unable to slip inside like this.

"Do you like to taunt me?" he growls in my ear, pressing his hips hard against me so I'm unable to move to find any relief. "You want some sort of reaction from me?"

"Maybe," I murmur.

"You liked me spanking your pussy, are you wanting me to find out if you like your ass spanked?"

I already know that I do, so I nod.

"Fuck, Spence, I never knew what a filthy little girl you were. I knew you'd be perfect for me, but I never knew *this*."

I want to voice the same thought I have about him, but I'm unable to because his hand comes down on the side of my ass with a sharp slap. I gasp and try to move my hips to get some sort of friction, but I'm weighed down by the heavy hockey player on me.

"You do like it, don't you?" he asks right before his teeth graze the side of my neck.

I nod, "Yes. More."

"Hm," he hums, shifting back, removing his full weight off my back, tangling one hand in my hair, holding my head down to the mattress while his other hand comes down on my ass with two smacks in a row.

I moan into the mattress, my pelvis rubbing on the bed, but it's not even close enough to what I want. I need him to touch me, or for him to let me touch myself.

"I have such a dirty fucking girl, don't I?"

I try to nod, but his hand holding my head down makes it impossible. He slaps my ass a couple more times, I know the skin has to be blooming pink and all it's doing is making me wetter and more desperate.

"Are you wet for me? Are you ready to take my cock in your perfect little cunt?"

"Yes," my voice is muffled by the bed, but I know he hears me.

"I'm going to get you close just from spanking this tight ass. Then, I'm going to fuck you nice and rough until you come on my cock. Later, I'll fuck you slow, treat you like the perfect girl you are. But I'll always fuck you like you're mine."

"I am yours," I say quietly. I'm not sure if he hears me. I really am saying three different words, but I know I can't voice those yet. I've told him I loved him before, but it was different then, clearly in a platonic way and we both know it. So, I don't say it now and neither does he. Both knowing we will wait.

He removes his hand from the back of my head, but before I can lift it, he's yanking me off the end of the bed so my legs are dangling off it. Then he's doing exactly what he said he would and is spanking my ass in quick succession. I'm writhing and moaning at the sensation. I can't keep track of how many times he does it before he plunges two fingers inside me.

"You are so soaked from this, aren't you?" This time he doesn't let me answer as he pulls his fingers out and brings his hand down on me even more.

I'm grinding against the bed, and I feel myself building, getting close just like he wants me to.

"*Jared*," I choke out on a desperate plea.

"You ready for my cock?" he asks with one more sharp slap that has me crying out.

"Yes, *yes*. Please."

He grabs a pillow, shoving it under my hips to angle me a bit better before he presses himself at my entrance without pushing in yet. I'm too strung up and impatient that I push back onto him, not letting him tease either of us anymore.

"*Fuck* Spence, how do you feel even better each time?"

His hands grip my hips tightly, pulling back then shoving forward roughly. I scream into the mattress, but he doesn't let up. He's fucking me roughly. Just like he said he would. His skin slaps my sensitive backside with each powerful thrust. I'm gripping the sheets tightly as my orgasm barrels through me after less than a minute.

"That's it. Soak my dick, Superstar. Mark me as yours."

Once my release has let up, he pulls out of me, and I start to protest before he yanks us both down to the floor and adjusts me so I'm straddling him. His hands on my thighs and the way he's looking at me right now is like he's in awe. Like I'm not real and he has to hold on or I'm going to disappear.

I can't help it; I lean down to kiss him. Both to reassure him that I'm not going to disappear and also to remind myself he's really here. That this whole thing happening between us is real. Our tongues tangle together in a sensual dance. His grip on my thighs tightens and I reach back to grab his length and guide it back inside me.

The groan he lets out into my mouth has me wanting to hear more from him. I love how vocal he is, it makes me feel like he's as completely lost for me as I am for him. I push up on his chest, my hair falling around me as I look down at him.

Hard muscled chest beneath my hands, bright blue eyes looking up at me with hunger and emotion.

I slide down on him, until I'm completely seated, moaning at the depth and how perfectly full I feel with him like this.

"You are the most beautiful woman I've ever seen," he says softly, such a stark difference than the growly dominant man he's been in bed with me. But it's just like how Jared, my best friend, would speak to me.

"You are the most handsome man *I've* ever seen," I counter.

"Now ride my cock until I'm filling your cunt. You want my cum, don't you?"

And just like that the switch is flipped again. "Yes, I want it."

"Such a good fucking girl for me. Take it, Spence, it's all yours."

I lift up and slam back down on him, keeping my hands on his chest for leverage as I ride him roughly. Grinding my hips with every thrust and I feel myself building again. The way Jared's fingers are biting into my skin lets me know he's holding back, and I know he wants to take control.

Doubling my efforts to chase yet another orgasm I'm fucking him as hard as I can before he finally loses the battle with his control and starts thrusting up into me. Leaning back slightly to rest my hands on his thighs, meeting his hips with my own.

"That feels so good," I moan, throwing my head back, my hair tickling my back while it swings around me.

"You look *so* fucking good taking my cock like it was made for you," his grip moves to my hips as he starts guiding my movement. Pushing me back and forth with each thrust up.

Out of nowhere, my release hits me hard. I fall forward onto his chest with a scream as the orgasm wracks through my whole body. My limbs turn to jelly and my mind goes blank, the only thing I'm conscious of at this moment is the pleasure consuming my whole body.

Jared continues to fuck me as I lay boneless on top of him before he flips us so he's on top of me and fucks me even harder. I try to wrap my arms and legs around him to hold him as close as possible. It doesn't take long before his thrusts become jerky, and his groans become louder.

He comes with my name on his lips, and I feel his release inside me, which makes me feel like I have another smaller orgasm. Is that even a thing? A minigasm? I don't even know; my brain is completely mush.

He rolls off me, pulling me against him. His hands rubbing along my back is what brings me back to the present. We are both sweat soaked and sticky, my body is draped across his and I don't think I can move for the next three to five business days.

"You okay?" he asks. The vibration of his chest underneath my cheek has me nuzzling more into him. I would crawl inside his skin if I could.

"I think so," I mumble.

He chuckles. "Maybe we should move to the bed."

"Mm, no I'm okay right here."

"You might be, but I think my back is going to have some issues if we sleep on the floor."

I groan, knowing he's right, but still not wanting to move. Luckily, I don't have to because with an impressive show of some strength and skill he lifts me into his arms while getting up and moving us both to the bed.

We settle under the covers, Jared holding me against him, my head resting on his chest with his arm wrapped around my shoulder. Even though I'm exhausted I force my eyes to stay open as I run my fingers across his chest tracing the hard lines of muscles there.

I think he's fallen asleep, so I say his name softly.

"Hm?" he responds, tightening his grip on my shoulder slightly.

"Are you asleep?"

"No. Are you?"

I giggle, turning my head into his chest more. "I was just thinking."

"Uh oh, that can't be good. Thinking about what?"

I look up at him, needing to see his face. The look in his

eyes as he stares down at me. I also blame my overly fucked brain for what comes out of my mouth. "Do I even want to know how you learned to fuck like that?"

He bites back a smile, "I don't know. Do you?"

I scrunch up my face thinking of Jared with other girls. I know he has been, obviously. We haven't ever shared that part of our lives with each other. But I know of exactly two Jared has had. Both were in high school. I'm not naïve enough to think he never hooked up with anyone since then. He's a hot, successful professional athlete. I'm sure he has a list of past hookups as big as Mount Everest.

I don't even know why I bring this up, clearly, I don't want to know.

"No, probably not."

He holds me closely against his chest, looking down at me with so much emotion that I can't bear to dissect right now.

"It's not as bad as you think. And just so you know, it's never been like this with anyone else. Not even close."

I can't help but smile, unsure of what else to say. Everything I'm thinking would be too much right now, so I stay quiet and it doesn't take long before I've drifted off, surrounded completely by Jared.

12

COLVER
30

I'm not sure what time it is when I wake up, but it's still dark when I feel warmth enveloping my cock. Moaning I don't even open my eyes yet because if this is a dream, it's the best fucking dream I think I've ever had. And after my night with Spencer, I can't help but feel like this is my mind continuing it for me and I never want it to end.

Except, the warmth is just around my tip, and then covering me about halfway down my shaft and I'm realizing this isn't a dream.

Reaching down I'm met with silky hair and vibration that has me tightening my grip and groaning out, "*Fuck.*"

She swallows more of me, and it takes all my effort not to come right this second.

"Good morning, Superstar," I manage to say through gritted teeth.

She hums around me again before popping me from her mouth, licking around the crown and smiling up at me. "Good morning."

I press my thumb to her bottom lip, already swollen, probably from last night and now this morning. "You know, you kind of stole my idea. I was going to wake you up with my mouth on you."

"Guess next time you'll have to wake up before me."

"I think I have a better idea." I pull her up my body, even though she protests. I press a chaste kiss to her mouth before maneuvering her so she's kneeling above my head. "Finish what you started while I have a morning snack."

I pull down on her thighs, until her pussy is on my mouth, so wet just from blowing me and I am addicted to her sweet taste. She takes a moment before finally leaning forward to take me back into her mouth hesitantly.

"I don't know how you expect me to focus when you're doing *that*," she says right before leaning forward and licking a line up my dick.

"You can handle it," I tell her before plunging my tongue inside her delicious pussy.

It hasn't taken me long to figure out exactly what to do to drive her wild. She's so responsive to everything I give her, but I get the best reaction when I flick her clit with my tongue a couple times teasingly then suck it hard. And how she responded to her pussy being spanked...*fuck*. That's not something I'll forget, ever.

She's not the only one distracted by her task because the way her hot mouth moves over me, and her tongue curls over my head has me holding back my release in a way that's almost painful. Add in the taste, smell, and feel of her cunt on my mouth and I'm about to explode. But she needs to come first.

With a growl I wrap my hands tighter around her thighs, pulling her down against my face. It doesn't take long before she's pressing harder against me. Her mouth isn't working me anymore, but it only makes me more determined to get her to explode on my tongue.

She's chanting my name, getting louder and louder and when I manage to press my thumb against her asshole, but not pressing in, she comes with a gush. I lap at her release coating my mouth. Her cries increase when I lick her completely to get everything I can from her.

"Too much," she whines when I don't let up from her overstimulated clit.

"Sorry, I can't help it. You taste too good," I tell her with another long lick up her entire center.

"So do you," she breathes before swallowing my shaft into her throat again.

Reflexively, my hips buck up further into her throat. I'm worried for a split second that move was too much for her, but the way she moans around me and grips my thighs even tighter I can tell she likes it.

"You like your throat fucked, dirty girl?"

"Mhm," she agrees, pulling back to just my tip before diving back down to take as much as she can.

I decide then I need more. Plus having her pussy still in my face is tempting beyond belief. I grip her hips and lift her up off me, setting her on the bed. I move to stand on the side of it, looking down at her with a smile on her red swollen lips, flushed skin and tear rimmed eyes.

"Come over here and take what you want," I tell her, and she hops up onto her knees on the bed before swallowing me again.

My head falls back with my groan. I slide my hands in her hair, tangling the soft strands through my fingers. "Tap my thigh twice if it's too much for you, okay?"

She pulls off my cock, looking up at me, "Okay."

Then she's taking me back in her mouth and I take over with my grip on her hair as I do what we both want and fuck her mouth. She keeps a grip on my thighs, nails biting into my skin, but she doesn't tap. She takes everything I give her just like she always does.

I'm so close, and I warn her. Even though I want to come down her throat and watch her swallow everything I give her. I want to see her marked by me more.

"I'm going to come on your face, Spence."

She hums and nods, gripping me tighter through my last couple thrusts before I'm pulling out of her warm mouth. I grip my cock, jerking myself until I'm shooting ropes of cum onto her gorgeous face, mouth open and tongue out.

As soon as I'm done, I grip her jaw and watch as she licks her lips, collecting the cum that landed there and swallowing.

"*Fuck* you're perfect," I scoop her into my arms and take her to the bathroom, starting the shower and bringing us both into it before it's even warmed up.

I press her against the tile wall to warm her with my body heat while we are pelted with the cold water. It starts to warm, but I don't move. My eyes are locked on hers as I really absorb the fact that she's here with me. That she's *mine*. That I love the woman standing in front of me and I always have.

Cupping her face, I press my lips to hers softly, because this isn't a kiss to take things further. This is a kiss to show her how I feel without saying it. She knows. I know she can tell, but I want to show her. I swipe my tongue across her bottom lip before pulling back, resting my forehead against hers.

"Let's get you cleaned up, then back to bed for a couple more hours of sleep."

"How about we never leave?" she counters, voice rough from the rawness of her throat. Luckily, I know she doesn't have to sing today.

"You want to live in a hotel with me?" I chuckle.

Shrugging, "They can bring us food and clean the room for us. Seems like a good setup."

"I mean, we can have that at one of our houses, too," I tease. It's no mystery we both make a significant amount of money. We could each afford those things on our own, and certainly could together.

"Good point," she sighs as she sags against me as I pull us into the, now, warm water. We stand with our bodies pressed completely together just letting the water run over us. "When do you have to go back home?"

I hug her tighter against me. I hate that my home isn't the same as her home, and I don't mean the same house. We don't even live in the same state right now. Of course, when I'm not in season I can live anywhere since I'm sure she has to be in L.A. whenever she's not touring.

"I have to be back in time for morning skate tomorrow," I tell her, reluctantly.

"I could..." her voice trails off and she smothers her face in my chest, cutting off her words.

I don't let her hide, guiding her face up with a light grip on her neck. "You could what, Superstar?"

"I could come with you," she practically whispers, and I barely hear her over the sound of the water. Then her words come out in a panicked rush, "I mean it would only be for a couple days, I go to Tennessee for my next show this weekend, but I have no reason to go back home and maybe – "

I cut her off with my lips on hers. I swear I'm addicted to her mouth. It's like now that I've gotten a taste, I can't stand looking at her for more than a few minutes without kissing the life out of her. Ending the kiss, reluctantly, I speak against her mouth, "Of course you can come back with me."

She beams up at me, yanking me back down to kiss her again. And because her mouth isn't the only thing I've become addicted to when it comes to Spencer, I take her again. This time slower, lifting her into my arms, pressing her back into the tile of the shower and fucking her slowly. Our mouths stay locked on each other even as the pleasure takes over both of us and we come at the same time.

The water is cold again by the time we get out of the shower, but I bundle her in a thick towel, drying every part of her body. Then, we fall into bed, both completely naked and fall asleep wrapped around each other like we never plan to let go.

13

SPENCER

Brynn was on board with coming back to Denver with Jared and me. Despite what she says about how annoyed she can get with her brother, I know she likes spending time with him. I know they come from a big family with shitty parents and that Brent, who's the oldest, practically raised his younger siblings.

I also know they lost one of their brothers to an overdose two years ago. She doesn't talk about it or him much. Occasionally she talks about her other two siblings Bryson and Bailey, but I know she's closest to Brent. Though, she insists she can't stay at his house and has to get a hotel.

We are all on the plane when that topic comes up.

"Why not?" I ask her.

"There's four of them in that relationship. I would never judge, and I love Chandler, but the last thing I need to be privy to is any noises that happen in that house," she shudders with her whole body.

"I remember when that all came out, everyone on the team was so confused," Jared adds.

"Were the guys assholes about it?" I ask him.

He shakes his head, "No. Not at all. The media was, but none of us particularly care what our teammates do in their bed." He sends a wink in my direction, and I drop my head when I feel the blush cover my cheeks.

"And this is why I won't stay at *your* house either," Brynn nods toward both of us.

"No idea what you're talking about. I'm a saint. And for the record I'm saving myself for marriage," Jared kicks his leg up so his ankle rests on his knee while he leans back in the seat.

I roll my eyes at him.

"Oh, uh huh, sure," Brynn glares at him jokingly.

∼

After getting to Jared's house and then proceeding to spend as much time as we could in bed, Jared had to go to practice this morning. I tried to convince him to stay, even though I knew he wouldn't. He told me he would be gone for a couple hours and that they have a game tonight. I also found out they have another game against L.A. the day before I have to go to Tennessee. This time it's on Denver's home ice and I'm glad I get to go. Especially considering I'm expecting a bloodbath.

Tensions are high between those two teams without adding the personal issues into it.

After I make some coffee and a small breakfast for myself, I stare at my phone on Jared's kitchen counter like it's going to explode any second. It's a landmine I haven't wanted to touch, I'm too happy in my bubble with Jared and pretending that the outside world doesn't exist. The pressures of my career, the media, and of course the conversation I need to attempt to have with Kenneth are stressing me out.

Brynn said I should try calling him, but the last thing I want to do is hear his voice. Somehow, I've convinced myself that if I do then he's intruding in my happy bubble and I'm not going to give him that. So, instead I sent him a text.

> Spencer: We need to talk.

It doesn't take him long to respond, which surprises me since I figured he would be at practice right now.

> Kenneth: I can come by later this afternoon.

> Spencer: I'm not home.

> Kenneth: Where are you?

I gnaw at my bottom lip, not wanting to tell him. Not because I care about his feelings or anything like that. Just because I don't want to hear whatever opinion he has on the matter. I want to get this all sorted publicly, like Brynn wants for me and not deal with the bullshit that is Kenneth Richardson.

Fuck it. I'm going to have to deal with it one way or another.

> Spencer: Denver.

This time his reply doesn't come as quickly. I bet he's fuming, drawing a conclusion that is most definitely correct. Jared never told me exactly what went down on the ice between them, but it's safe to assume it at least partly had to do with me. And they've never liked each other the entire time I was with Kenneth anyway.

> Kenneth: With him?

I roll my eyes.

> Spencer: It doesn't matter. We need to talk so we can put this all behind us.

> Kenneth: I'll call you once I'm home.

I know he's trying to get me to question where he is, but I couldn't give less of a fuck, so with that I leave him on read.

Jared lets me know the team is having a review session of some tape and then a meeting, so he won't be home for a couple hours. As disappointing as that is for me, I've been using this alone time in his house to write the music that has been on repeat in my mind. The inspiration is flowing from me, just like the song I played for him. It's like the lock on my creativity has been obliterated. It's certainly something I can get used to.

When my phone rings I get an excited pang thinking it's going to be Jared telling me he's on his way home, but unfortunately, it's the last person I want to talk to. I almost let it go to voicemail, until I remember *why* he's calling. And that I need to get this done.

"Hi," I answer, curtly.

Kenneth sighs on the other end of the phone. "I thought you might pretend to be excited to talk to me. Especially after ignoring me for weeks."

"Oh, you mean ignoring your useless pleas to talk to me after *you* went to the media and said we broke up. Instead of, uh, I don't know, *telling me?*" I'm not even mad about that, I'm mad that he thinks I owe him any niceness.

"Yes, because then I could have explained that wasn't what it looks like and was all my teams doing. I didn't want to break up with you, Spencer. I love you, you know that."

I hold back a gag. "No, you don't. You loved what I did for your image, but you didn't *love* me. We've been over for a while Kenny," he hates to be called that. "I just didn't know how to fully end it, but you took care of that for me. So, thank you."

He scoffs, "Oh, were we over for a while because you started fucking that goalie? I always knew your story of being such good friends was bullshit."

"You think I cheated on you? Is that going to be the next thing you run and tell the tabloids?" I probably shouldn't goad him like this, and I know if Brynn were here, she would not appreciate the approach I'm taking since I'm supposed to be convincing him to issue a *mutual* statement.

"I don't give a shit about telling them, but it's pretty fucking obvious and I think anyone with a brain would be able to figure it out."

"Think what you want, I just want to get you out of my life and have us both issue a mutual statement that we amicably split and move the fuck on."

"Amicable," he sneers.

"Yes. It means agreeing to something which I know is tough for you."

He laughs. Loudly. "I get it. You don't want anyone to see you as the bad guy in this."

"I want you to do one decent thing in your life and not make this complicated."

"Maybe if you had talked to me when I first reached out to you, I would have cared more about what you want. But after you made sure your new little boyfriend went after me, I don't give a shit what you want anymore."

"Fuck you, Kenny. I don't know why I wanted to try to talk to you. I don't know why I was even with you for so long. Say what you want about me, I don't care. I can handle it. As long as I'm not having to deal with you anymore, I'll take whatever hate comes my way."

I hang up the phone, not even caring to hear his response. Then for extra measure I block his number. For years I bit my tongue around him, not wanting to deal with the confrontation. I just assumed maybe it would get better and then at some point I realized I didn't care if it would or not. I stayed out of convenience and now that I'm free I'm not looking back.

Consequences be damned.

. . .

Brynn is going to kill me.

~

I was right.

Brynn is currently yelling at me over the phone when Jared walks in. He gives me a wide smile, approaching me with purpose until he clearly hears the yelling on the other end of the phone. Then he stops within arm's reach of me, but doesn't touch me and I wish he would.

I keep giving Brynn placating noises of "Uh huh," "yup," and "I know."

"I know you were mad. I'm mad too, and part of me can't blame you for what happened because I get it, I do. But *fuck* Spencer, if he tries to drag you through the mud it's going to take a fucking firehose to clean up your image."

"I know," I say for the tenth time. This is publicist Brynn. And I get why this side of her is upset with me, even though I know as my friend she's pretty proud of what I did.

Jared looks at me, concerned. I reach out to tug on his hand, pulling him to wrap his arms around me. I need his warmth and comfort right now.

"We will handle it just like we always do. First, I'm going to type up a statement for you to post before he comes out with your slander campaign. I want you to post it as soon as I send it. No distractions, especially of the dick variety. Got it?"

I can't stop the laugh that bubbles out, I try to smother it in Jared's chest, but I know she hears. "Okay. No distractions until the statement is posted."

"Thank you. Talk to you soon."

We hang up, I toss my phone onto the couch, wrap my arms around Jared's middle and look up at him with a wide smile, trying to forget the annoying, chaotic morning I've had.

"What was that about? Is everything okay?" he asks.

I sigh, resting my forehead against his chest, "Not exactly."

Pulling him to sit next to me on the couch I proceed to rehash the conversation with Kenneth, Brynn's original plan, and where we stand right now. The entire time I'm talking I watch him restrain his obvious anger. In the middle of my retelling I get the text from Brynn with my statement. I post it right away before continuing. By the time I'm done I'm holding his hands that are vibrating with the need to break Kenneth's face.

"I'm going to kill him."

14

COLVER 30

After what Spencer told me, how Kenneth spoke to her. I knew he was a piece of shit, and I even know some of the rough moments from when they were together. But this has me seeing red. I may have gotten to hit him during the last game, but it's not enough.

"Hey, it's going to be handled. I want to kill him too, but the best thing we can do is *thrive*. Even if he starts all sorts of rumors about me, the best revenge we can have is being unbothered and living our best lives."

Looking at her, she's so sure, and I feel like anyone else in her position would be terrified about what is potentially about to happen to their reputation. But not Spencer. She knows it'll be handled. She's so confident and sure of who she is and knows that she will rise above this. That we both will because she knows I'll be by her side the entire way.

God, I love her. I love her so fucking much. I respect the hell out of her, and it makes me love her more. I want to tell her. I want to lay my feelings out in front of her right now. Drop down to my knees, confess everything and then worship her entire body.

I know if I tried to do that I would seem like a frantic crazy person. Instead, I go with a softer approach, taking her hands in mine, bringing her fingertips to my lips to press soft, barely there kisses to them.

"I know it'll all work out. And I'm here for you through it all," I tell her, seriously.

The unspoken words hang between us. We both feel it, I know we do, but neither of us say them. Instead, she swings her leg over my lap, straddling me before kissing me so deeply we are ripping each other's clothes off in no time.

Once we are naked, she's guiding me inside her and this time as she sinks down on me it's like when I took her in the shower. Slow, savoring each other instead of fucking with a frenzy like we are running out of time.

"Fuck, baby, there is nothing better than you riding my cock," I rasp against the skin of her neck as she rotates her hips.

"Nothing feels better than riding your cock," she moans, pulling my mouth up to hers to kiss me deeply.

I grip her hips tightly as my need to fuck her harder increases. I want to let her control this, but it's getting harder and harder by the second. Watching her tits bounce with each movement. The way her pussy grips me, so fucking tight.

"Jared," her voice is a breathy moan against my open mouth.

"Spence," I drag my lips along her neck, nipping her skin as I make my way to her shoulder, then lower where I lick one of her pointed nipples. She grips my hair tightly.

"Fuck me. Hard. Please."

My teeth sink into the skin of her breast, pulling her nipple into my mouth causing her to cry out and yank my hair harder. I do the same to her other nipple but continue to let her ride me at her pace, which has increased slightly.

"Jared, *please*," she begs. I pull my lips off her nipple, admiring how red and pointed they both are now. My eyes trail up to her face where she's panting, eyes pleading while her hips continue to work me.

"If you insist," I attack her mouth, my tongue lapping at hers as my arms wrap around her waist and I flip her onto her back on the couch, never once leaving her body.

She squeals at the movement and I'm hovering over her, holding my body weight off her with my hands planted by her head. "How hard do you want me to fuck you?" I taunt, pulling out slightly. She wraps her legs around my back and tries to pull me back.

"As hard as you can," she smirks.

"You sure?" I lean down, biting her bottom lip, then soothing the bite with my tongue.

She nods. "Fuck me like I'm yours."

So, I do. Pulling out so just my tip is inside her; I watch where our bodies are connected before slamming forward so hard, she screams, and grips me tighter. I would have thought it was too much if she wasn't already chanting, *"yes."*

I do what she asks, and I fuck her like she's mine. Because she is. I take both her hands in one of mine, holding them above her head by her wrists, keeping them there while I pound into her. Spencer screams not to stop, how good it feels. I continue to praise her as I feel the telltale signs of her getting close.

"Fuck, Spencer, come on my cock. You're so perfect, you take me so well. Soak my dick, come baby."

And she does. She comes, screaming as I muffle the sound with my mouth on hers as my movements become jerky and I feel my own orgasm approaching. I let go of her hands and they immediately go to my back, nails digging into my skin. I groan as my release barrels through me, and I'm coming for what feels like forever.

When it finally feels like it's subsided, I pull out of her to watch my release drip from her cunt.

"Fuck, that's such a pretty sight, Spence."

She giggles, her body limp, flushed and fucking beautiful.

After, I clean her up and we've settled back on the couch. I don't have long before I need to leave for my game tonight, but I'm savoring every second I can with her. I think she's dozed off, leaning against me with her head resting on my chest and my arm wrapped around her. Her breathing has evened out and that's when I say the words I've been holding back, but don't want to say too soon.

"I love you, Spencer," I whisper so I don't wake her up.

She shoots up and my heart starts pounding against my ribcage. She's looking at me wide eyed and I probably look similar.

"What?" she squeaks out.

"Uh, I thought you were sleeping," I stammer.

"Pretty sure even if I was, I would've woken up from that." I'm about to say something to try and make this better, but then she's smiling at me so wide I practically melt. "Say it again."

I cup her face, pulling her toward me, ghosting my lips over hers softly then repeating, "I love you."

She kisses me, then. Her lips are demanding against mine, tongue pushing into my mouth, and we are both panting by the time we pull apart and she says, "I love you too."

I can't help it, I take her mouth again, falling into each other and almost not giving a fuck if I end up missing my game tonight.

∽

HAVING Spencer at my house this week has been a fucking dream. She came to our last game, which we won on a shutout.

She gave me a reward for not letting a single goal in that included my cock in her mouth. Then I proceeded to worship her and fuck her senseless.

Every day I come back from practice my house is filled with music, but it's not music played on a speaker or anything. It's Spencer, working and writing. Sometimes she's practicing songs I already know. Sometimes it's something new she's working on. I always admire her, refusing to disrupt what she's doing because I love her determination, how focused and lost in the music she gets. That's how she's always been. Music is special to her, it has the ability to take her to another place mentally that's just hers.

Every night I show her how much I love her with our bodies. And now with our words since we've finally admitted it to each other. I never want her to leave. I know it's selfish of me because she's on tour and has fans she needs to make happy. But fuck do I want her all to myself.

I'm in the locker room and it's the last game before she leaves. Plus, it's against the L.A. Spartans again. So, tensions are high with my entire team as everyone does their pre-game rituals. I'm mentally preparing for anything Spencer's ex thinks he's going to pull out there. Again. And hoping I can hold back from beating his ass the second I see him. I've always enjoyed being a goalie, but this is the first time I wish maybe I played a different position so I would have free reign to let loose on that asshole.

Coach already talked to me and asked if he should put our backup goalie in tonight for me. I just scoffed. I may have told him it would all be okay, but I doubt he believed me. I didn't believe myself either.

During warmups I look up at the suite where I know Spencer is. It's so high up I can't exactly see her, but I can feel her eyes on me. My mask covers almost my whole face so she can't see me either, but it doesn't hinder the connection we have, even from a distance.

The game starts and I'm on fire, blocking every shot that comes my way. Sliding across the ice to catch a flying puck headed for the top shelf of the goal. My legs splitting while stopping a slap shot from one of the L.A. players. My defensemen are killing it, helping prevent too many shots coming to me, or slowing them down to help me out.

It doesn't take long before Kenneth and I have a run in. The first one came as he stopped a little too close to me, spraying ice all over my mask as I smother the puck with my glove. I flip the puck up and catch it again as the ref skates over to take it from me. Kenneth takes the pause in the game to start on his bullshit.

"Heard Spencer's been staying with you; hope you've been enjoying her pussy. She was always a bit boring, but nice to look at."

"The fuck did you just say?" I spit out, reaching up to remove my helmet when my teammate, Dumont, comes over stopping me by stepping between us.

"Don't start shit right now, just ignore him," Dumont tells me, but I can't even look at him. I'm staring at Kenneth's retreating form as his own teammate pushes him away.

"You didn't hear what he said, and you would beat his ass if he said that about Chandler," I tell him. I know how protective he is of her too.

"You're probably right about that, but we need you out here and you know it's different if you get ejected. Just ignore him and we got you." He pats my shoulder, jostling my pads before skating over to his position for the puck drop.

I squirt a stream of water into my mouth through my mask before getting into position myself, then the play begins again. We win the face off and they take the puck to the other end of the ice. I watch every movement to be prepared in case there's a breakaway from the other team that sends them back my way.

My teammates score, putting us at one to zero. When we score first it always gets me fired up and even more determined to get us a shutout. As the next play starts, my teammate, Mann, gets a two-minute penalty for cross checking putting us in a penalty kill. I prepare for us to be outnumbered for the duration of Mann being stuck in the box.

My team is doing a great job killing their power play, but then the Spartans get into our zone on the ice and start attempting shots. I block each and every one that comes at me. I'm sweating too much, it's dripping into my eyes when the special sound signals when their player comes back onto the ice and ending of the Spartans' power play.

The game continues with several more calls for various penalties. McQuaid on my team gets into it with some guy on the Spartans and they both get two minutes for roughing. I can't control my laughter when Kenneth gets called for interference.

Unfortunately, at the end of the second period one of the L.A. players fakes me out and is able to get a goal past me. I'm pissed I missed it, and then we are heading into the locker room for the last intermission. I don't talk to anyone, keeping my focus because now we are going into the third period tied and I don't want us having to go into overtime. I just want to end this.

The one thing I'm somewhat thankful for is the lack of confrontation from Kenneth. He also hasn't had much of a chance to do or say anything else to me with the game being so fast paced, but it's not over yet.

The final period starts, and both our teams are out for blood trying to win this. My guys get it over to the Spartans zone, attempting a few shots that miss or get blocked. L.A. gets it out of their zone and over to ours, so it's my turn to block. This continues throughout the period, but then Kenneth is skating toward me, puck on his stick and he doesn't fucking stop. Instead of shooting from a normal distance he gets as close to me as he can, almost copying the exact move he did the last game. But this time, instead of turning at the last minute he collides with me, sending me tumbling back into the goal.

I hear him laughing as he gets up, and I lose it. Throwing my gloves and helmet down I grab him by the jersey, throwing him onto the ice and start punching him. There are whistles going off, the crowd going wild, sticks hitting the ice, my teammates getting into it with the other team, but I don't care. I'm focused on how it feels when my knuckles collide with Kenneth's face.

"You'll never speak to or about Spencer. Ever. Fucking. Again." I punctuate each word with another hit. I feel someone trying to pull me off the guy, but I resist it to keep raining down the punches. He keeps grappling with my jersey, but I'm much more padded than him so he's unable to get a good grip. He does get in a couple good hits to my face. I taste the blood in my mouth, but I just smile with each punch I land on him.

"That's enough," I'm yanked up by two refs. "You're done. Out."

"Fuck you, Richardson," I spit at him as he gets up, wiping the blood from his face. He still smirks at me like he has the upper hand here. It makes me want to go after him again.

I storm back to the locker room, not even looking at anyone as I head back, obviously I'm out of the game. Probably suspended for a couple of them if I'm honest. If not by the NHL, then by Coach for sure. It was worth it, at least it felt good. I'm sure Richardson will have some sort of repercussion as well, but I don't give a fuck.

For a brief moment I wonder if Spencer is going to be mad, but then I remembered she wasn't last time. In fact, if I remember correctly she *liked* it. I'm just hoping she will appreciate it again. I throw off my gear, not giving a fuck about any of it because I'm still keyed up, pissed off and wanting to erase that prick from our lives.

"Jared?" I hear the soft raspy voice that I would know anywhere.

I'm shirtless, just in my goalie pants, and leg pads and skates still on as I turn toward her. She gasps at my appearance. I'm not even sure what I look like other than the taste of blood in my mouth and that my knuckles burn.

She rushes toward me, reaching up to inspect my face before taking my hand in hers and looking at my busted knuckles. My eyes don't follow hers, I'm too focused on watching her and waiting for a reaction.

"Are you okay?" she asks, looking up at me.

I nod, unable to say anything, I think because I'm worried about her possible reaction. My mind is distracted, still simmering with anger.

"Good, because I think that was the hottest thing I've ever witnessed and the only reason I'm not jumping you right this second is because the period is almost over, and we will be caught."

"Wait, what?" I look into her bright green eyes, shocked by *that* being her response. Again.

She loops her arms around my neck, yanking me down to her to kiss me, I groan the second our mouths make contact from the twinge of pain there, but it is soothed by her tongue swiping across my bottom lip. Not even caring about the blood which should gross me out, but I'm too worked up to care. I crush her body to mine, but she pulls back before we get too carried away. I'm so out of it, I would, without thinking twice.

"I love you. I'll meet you outside after you're done in here,'" she beams up at me, smacking one last kiss on my mouth before escaping the locker room right before the final buzzer goes off.

The guys come in, pissed off because L.A. got a goal on our

backup goalie. I was too distracted in my own head with Spencer to hear anything going on out there. I want to be pissed with them, and part of me is. But I know I get to enjoy Spencer for one more full night before she has to go to her next tour stop. And I got to beat the shit out of her ex, so I'm pretty pleased with myself.

15

SPENCER

After I leave the locker room I'm waiting in the hallway, tucked away in an area that isn't as obvious. Brynn is talking to someone who works with the team, and I know she will be pissed when she realizes what I'm about to do.

With my statement posted a couple days ago about my mutual split with Kenneth saying that it's for the best. That neither of us will make any comments on the matter and to respect our privacy at this time. I decide I'm not wanting to tiptoe or try to hide anything with Jared just to please Kenneth and his precious feelings.

That's why I opened up a picture I took of Jared and my hands clasped together while we were sitting on his couch. I put a black and white filter on it, then I post it on social media with two heart emojis. One white and one black. Nothing else. Then, I shut off my phone.

When I look up the L.A. players are walking through, I tuck

further back so Kenneth doesn't see me, and luckily, he doesn't. But my attention is drawn to another player when he shouts, "Brynn baby!"

My eyebrows draw together as I watch him approach Brynn. Fully interrupting her conversation, he drapes his arm around her shoulders for a second before she shoves him off. "Get the fuck away from me, you don't even know me."

"No, but you know I want to," he flirts. I watch the interaction enthralled with what is happening. It's Colton.

"Never going to happen. Run along," she actually shoos him away and I muffle my laughter.

"Keep playing hard to get, it only makes the chase more exciting for me."

Brynn makes an exaggerated gagging noise as he walks away. I file this whole interaction away to ask her about later. She finishes her conversation shortly after that and comes over to me.

"Hey, I assume you're leaving with Jared?" She isn't upset about it or anything, but I can sense the underlying annoyance from Colton.

"Yeah, I know we have to fly out in the morning."

"Try not to conveniently sleep in or anything," she teases me with a wink, and I chuckle.

"I'll try." She gives me a hug and leaves shortly before Jared comes out in the fitted suit he's changed into.

"Hey," he says. I see his hand twitch with the desire to reach out to me, but he's holding back, clearly unsure if he should. I take the choice away from him and launch myself into his arms.

I wrap my arms around his neck, and he wraps his arms around my waist as I'm lifted in the air while I kiss him almost desperately. I don't care who sees. I don't care how this may look. In this moment I don't care about any of the outside noise. I just care about this time I have with him.

He pulls back with a smile; I can see the cut on his lip now that he's cleaned up. "Ready to go?"

I nod and he puts me down, linking our hands together as we walk out to the garage together. Getting into his car, we drive back to his house. I take in the sights as he drives, the snow-covered buildings and streets, thinking about if I could live here. Denver is beautiful. I can write and record music almost anywhere. Fly to L.A. whenever I need, but I don't need to live there like he needs to live here.

Glancing over at Jared he looks more relaxed than he did before. His body lax in the seat and I take him in. His muscular frame covered in the suit he wore for game day. For a moment, I think about all the bullshit that went down with Kenneth and I'm sure it's not over, especially after tonight. Brynn will probably have her work cut out for her on my behalf. But for right now I'm going to enjoy staring at the hot as fuck man currently sitting next to me.

"What are you looking at?" he asks with a teasing tone without making eye contact with me.

"You," I answer honestly.

"Like what you see?" he looks over at me with an exaggerated smolder.

I snort out a laugh, "Not anymore."

"Whatever. You love me."

Nodding, I agree, "Yeah, I do."

∼

WE BARELY MADE it inside Jared's house with our clothes on because I attempted to jump him in the car, but he insisted he needed more room than the front seat of his car to fuck me like I deserved to be fucked. We stumbled inside with fabric being shed along the way to his bedroom. He went down on me for what felt like forever, I swear I don't even know how many times I came because they seemed to just run together, and I was just a mess of pleasure before he even fucked me.

When he did, it's like he took out every ounce of leftover aggression from the ice on my body as he moved inside me. I came at least three more times before he finally let go himself.

We lay in a heap of sweat and cum on his bed, neither of us able to move, holding each other loosely. Even though I'm exhausted, I refuse to go to sleep because I don't want my time with him to end any sooner than it has to. If I go to sleep, then I'll wake up and have to leave.

"Spencer," he says my name gently with a sweep of his fingertips up my arm that makes me shiver.

"Yeah?" My throat is raw from all the noise I was making, but drinking some honey lemon tea has seemed to become my ritual when I'm around Jared because I'm either sore from screaming or sucking his massive cock.

"I hope you know that I'm all in with you. I hate that we are about to be apart, but distance has never mattered when we were just friends and it's not going to matter now that we are together." He continues to trail his fingertips along my arm as he speaks.

I sit up slightly to look at him. "I wasn't planning on it being any other way. You said I was yours, and I wasn't changing that."

"Good, you're stuck with me." He pulls me down, tightly against his chest and I laugh.

"Oh, you're definitely stuck with me. I may or may not have posted a photo earlier that drags you into my world officially."

"What did you post?" he doesn't sound upset, just curious.

"That picture of our hands. It could've been anyone, but I tagged you because I wanted it clear that I'm with *you*. Brynn will kill me for not running it by her first, but I don't care. I wanted the world to know I'm yours."

Jared rolls me onto my back, hovering over me, looking down at me with a wide smile. I'm sure I have one that is similar. "Have I told you I love you?" he jokes.

"Hm, no I don't think you have. Maybe you should."

"I love you," he kisses the tip of my nose, "I love you," the corner of my mouth, "I love you," just below my ear, "I love you," my neck.

I'm laughing and pull him up to look at me again. "I get it, you love me, god you're so obsessed." I dramatically roll my eyes.

"Oh, you're going to get it," he nuzzles his face into the side of my neck so I'm screaming with laughter. "Say it back."

I struggle to speak through my hysterical laughter, "I love you, *gah*, stop."

He lifts up again to look down at me, "Good. Now," in a quick move he's shifting slightly and flipping me onto my stomach, slapping my ass then pulling my hips up and angling himself behind me, "I'm going to spend the rest of the night fucking you so that when you get on that plane tomorrow, you're going to be sore and pumped full of my cum, so you remember that."

Then he pushes inside me and does exactly that. The man I've loved for so long. My best friend. My everything. I know this is just the beginning for us. We have forever to look forward to.

To be continued in Brynn's book "The Break Out" Coming late 2024

NEXT IN THE HAT TRICK SERIES

The Power Play
A forced proximity hockey romance.

If you want to read the first chapter of Audrey and Charlie's book, keep reading.

THE POWER PLAY
AUDREY

I finish the last touches of my makeup before sliding the lace mask over my eyes, taking one last look at myself. My shoulder length black hair is pulled back under my long purple wig and my dark lipstick draws attention to my mouth. I smile to make sure it looks genuine, right before crossing off the last item on my to do list written in dry erase marker on my mirror.

I look into my eyes in the mirror while I say my affirmations, "I am so lucky, everything works out for me." I repeat the phrase three times as I always do. "Let's do this," I tell myself before heading into the second bedroom of my townhouse I recently converted into my cam room.

My best friend, Chandler, used to have this room to herself, but when she moved out with her three boyfriends – lucky bitch – I was able to redesign it as my dream cam room. When I walk into this room, I'm no longer Audrey. In here, I'm Lacey Hale, and she's who my viewers know. They may think it's who

I really am, but I'm a great actress, and they don't know me at all. That's why this is a job.

I go through my pre-show checklist I have set up by the mounted TV so it's out of view from the camera, but in view for me. It's next to the list of predetermined "items" people can pay for which is what they can tip me, and I'll do for them. Somewhat like a performer monkey, only sexier.

Once I'm ready, camera angle adjusted, ambient lighting on, and my toys are all cleaned and prepped, I post to my followers that I'm about to go live right before opening my virtual "room." I have a couple of my regulars join almost right away, including those I have designated as moderators because bots are annoying. They pop into the comments promoting bullshit that isn't even real. Plus, some guys need to be kicked out when they get a bit too pushy.

I know what I do for a living, and I do love it, but harassment is harassment and it's not tolerated, especially in the sex work industry.

"Hi Robby. Hi Jon," I greet with a smile as I see two of my regulars join the room.

I make small talk with them for a little while and others as they come into the room. It isn't just sex with a lot of them, it's about the connection. Anyone can pull up a porn video to get off, that's not the point of watching a cam girl. This is about the connection along with the sexual elements.

Of course, I will end up performing sexual acts on camera, but sometimes it can be ten minutes after the start of the show or several hours. It all just depends. Then, there's also private rooms which people can request to have me alone for a while. For a significant fee.

> Robby: How was your day, gorgeous?

"It was good," I stretch my arms up above my head because part of this is to be enticing and show off parts of myself just enough to tease. I've basically mastered the art of it, and I'm pretty proud of that. "How about yours?"

I notice a few new people join the room, but they don't say anything. I used to greet everyone who came into my room, but quickly realized that is way too much work.

> Robby: Busy, but much better now that I get to see you.

I paste a big smile on my face, and subtly push my chest together with my arms. "Aw, you're too sweet to me. So, what all is everyone looking forward to?"

I watch as the messages come in, and of course there's the expected ones saying they are looking forward to me taking my clothes off, watching me ride a dick, sucking a dick. I don't pay too much mind to it, they can say what they want, but unless they pay me, they aren't going to see it.

"Well, I'm looking forward to hockey season starting. I have some tricks up my sleeve," I tell them. This was something Chandler and I came up with. I usually watch games with her, it's become a tradition, but we aren't able to watch them all so I figured I should have some fun when we can't be together.

I notice another familiar name join the room and I can't help the smile that spreads on my face at the name.

"Hi Charles," I greet.

> Charles: Hey pretty girl.

Charles is my longest regular and he was also my first. I had just started camming four years ago and he was the first to request a private show from me. I was extremely nervous and anticipated some guy old enough to be my dad saying creepy things to me while he got off. To my surprise when he turned his camera on, I couldn't see his face, only his bare chest that was surprisingly muscular.

That wasn't the only shocking part, the other was that we only talked. That first time. It was a short ten-minute video, and he didn't even ask me to take off my clothes. I figured that would be a one off and we'd never see each other again. But it wasn't. Of course, over the years we've had countless sexual calls and also nonsexual ones.

I'd say Charles is the closest thing I've had to a relationship.

Which is stupid to say considering he's a stranger online and I've never seen his face. He's never really seen mine either because I've always had my mask on.

But it's probably for the best that the only semi-real relationship I ever entertain is purely online.

> Jon: What team are you going to be rooting for?

"Denver Dragons, all the way. That's my team," I announce proudly. "Get ready for the shows while I watch hockey, I'll have prizes every time the Dragons score, if any of the guys get a penalty and the biggest prize will be when any player gets a hat trick."

A few more messages come in, some calling me their dream girl, some complaining that I'm not naked which I just ignore.

Then, a private request pops up, and I bite back my smile when I see it's Charles.

"Guys, I'll be back in a few, and then you can tell me what you're hoping to see from me tonight," I pause the room with a wink while I switch over to the private room.

It takes around thirty seconds to load, and I readjust myself, making sure my boobs are pushed up and paste a smile on my face for him to see right away.

"Hey handsome," I greet as his video loads before revealing Charles sitting how he usually does, leaning back revealing his bare chest and the top of his waistband.

"Hey pretty girl," his voice is so deep and it's embarrassing how those three words make me shiver.

"Did hearing me talk about hockey get you all hot and bothered?" I tease.

He chuckles, "Something like that. Sometimes I just can't help but steal you away to keep you for myself."

"Well, you know you're welcome to do that whenever you want," I flirt. "What are you wanting tonight?"

"I had something else in mind, but now I think I need to

hear about what you are thinking about for those hockey shows," he rests his large hand on his chest like he's getting comfortable, and I can't help but watch the movement. I've never been so tempted to touch someone over cam as I am when it comes to him.

I shake my head subtly to pull my thoughts away from one of the many fantasies I've conjured up over the years that include Charles. "I haven't fully planned it out yet, but what are you wanting to know?"

"Anything, I need to know what I'll be rooting for when I watch."

"Hm, well I'll probably have a list of things that will change with each game. For the first one, I'm thinking that each time the Dragons score I'll take off a piece of clothing," I tease the strap on my shoulder, pulling it down slightly but not removing it. "And if a Dragon player gets a penalty, I'll probably get a punishment, I'm thinking with one of my paddles."

"You know you'll have to do that a lot because of McQuaid."

"Oh, you *are* a fan then?"

"I never said I wasn't."

I give him a skeptical look because it sounds like he wants to say more, but I let it go. "I know that if any of the Dragons players get a hat trick then it immediately leads to the finale, and I get to come." I tell him with a wink.

"There better be a lot of hat tricks this season," he says, and even though I can't see his face I can tell he's smiling.

"If you ever talk to any of them you better tell them that."

"I will track the team down to make sure I tell them."

Preorder The Power Play - Releasing June 28, 2024

ALSO BY MADI DANIELLE

Hat Trick Series

The Hat Trick - A hockey why choose romance

The Power Play - Releasing June 28, 2024

The Break Out - Releasing late 2024 (Date on Amazon is a placeholder)

The Falling Series

When They Fell

Who They Are

What They Feel

ACKNOWLEDGMENTS

I have to start off by thanking my friends Ashley and Jenna who were my sounding boards when this idea came to me. I asked if I was crazy to write this while in the middle of writing another book. They encouraged the madness and here we are! I'm glad they did because Jared and Spencer wanted their sweet spicy story and I had so much fun writing it.

Also huge thank you to my editor, Kay, and cover designer Aliyah for helping me last minute when I told them what I was doing!

Thank you to Sarah Beth, as always you are the best and you can never get rid of me, so don't ever try!

Thank you to my beta readers! Especially when you catch my dumbass mistakes that I look back and question what was even going through my mind when I wrote some things.

Massive thank you to my readers. I can't believe the love you showed for The Hat Trick and this story and all the rest wouldn't exist without you all. Thank you times a million!

Get ready for Audrey and Brynn's stories. They are fun and spicy in different ways and I'm so excited to share.

ABOUT THE AUTHOR

Madi is 20 something trying to figure out what "adulting" is. Madi has been writing stories since she was a teenager she continues to express all her emotions in her writing. She's also an avid reader. Madi lives in the PNW where she attended college after moving from the unforgiving heat of Arizona. Madi spends her free time with her husband, daughter and family of pets (3 dogs and 2 cats).

Printed in Great Britain
by Amazon